HAVANA
is a really
BIG CITY

AND OTHER SHORT STORIES

HAVANA is a really BIG CITY

AND OTHER SHORT STORIES

by Mirta Yáñez

Edited by Sara E. Cooper

Cubanabooks

Copyright © by Mirta Yáñez and Cubanabooks

All rights reserved. Except for brief quotations in critical articles and reviews, no part of this book may be used or reproduced in any manner without written permission from the publisher.

Published in the United States of America by Cubanabooks.
400 W. 1st St., Dept. FLNG, CSUC, Chico, CA 95929-0825

Printed in the United States of America
Cover design: Krista Yamashita
Cover photo: Mirta Yáñez
Author photo: Miguel García Vidal
Text design: Kellen Livingston
Cubanabooks logo art: Krista Yamashita

First Edition
10 9 8 7 6 5 4 3 2 1

"We Blacks All Drink Coffee" appeared first in *Her True-True Name: An Anthology of Women's Writing from the Caribbean,* edited by Pamela Mordecai (Portsmouth, NH: Heinemann, 1990) and is reproduced here with permission.

"Go Figure" appeared first in *Out of the Mirrored Garden,* edited by Delia Poey (New York: Anchor Books/Doubleday, 1996) and is reproduced here with permission.

An earlier version of "The Blind Buffalo" appeared in *Remaking A Lost Harmony: Stories from the Hispanic Caribbean,* edited by Margarite Fernandez Olmos and Lizabeth Paravisini-Gebert (Buffalo, NY: White Pine Press, 1995) and is included here with permission.

Library of Congress Control Number: 2010931659

CONTENTS

Introduction	xii
The Mourner	1
The Escape	5
The Discovery	8
It's In Me Somewhere	13
For Men Only	19
We Blacks All Drink Coffee	24
Havana Is a Really Big City	28
Go Figure	37
The Beatles vs. Duran Duran	46
Kid Bururú and the Cannibals	59
Prophet of Dawn	67
The Blind Buffalo	78
No Call of the Wild	89
About the Translators	93

INTRODUCTION

Mirta Yáñez, born in Havana, Cuba, in 1947, is a *Cubana,* through and through—a strong, rebellious, funny, and articulate woman with a fierce love of her nation and creative freedom. Poet, novelist, critic, and extraordinary writer of short fiction, Yáñez is three-time winner of the coveted Critics' Prize in Cuba. Her narrative stands out by virtue of a complex, yet unmistakable, Cuban flavor and a characteristic preoccupation with the social, political, and economic particularities of the island and how these affect *los cubanos.* Her scrutiny results in the depiction of multiple facets of an intricate society that by turns has been exoticized, simplified, maligned, celebrated, and exaggerated in the literary production of the last half-century.

Garnering renewed popular and critical acclaim in Cuba since the release of a new edition of *El diablo son las cosas* in 2001, Yáñez arguably is the most important writer of her generation. Catherine Davies calls Yáñez one of the "most outstanding short story writers" among Cuban women, commenting that "Yáñez writes about everyday life in Havana; her chatty, colloquial style full of light-hearted humour, whatever the theme, makes her fiction a delight to read" (*Women* 154-155).[1] Aficionados of Cuban culture and general readers alike will be delighted with this collection of witty and ironic accounts of adventure, reflection, and epiphany in contemporary Cuba.

Havana Is a Really Big City reproduces the original seven stories published in Cuba as *La Habana es una ciudad bien grande* in 1980, adding six more recent tales that mirror a similar tone and literary style. "The Mourner" is a poignant treatment of the topic of death. Narrated in indirect discourse with interspersed snippets of remembered or

---

[1] Davies, Catherine. "Women Writers in Twentieth Century Cuba: An Eight-Point Survey." Gender and Genre in Caribbean Women's Writing. Ed. Joan Anim-Addo. London: Whiting & Birch, 1996. 138-58.

imagined dialogue, the story follows old Severino's path toward the cemetery and greater understanding of love, forgiveness, and pain. Entirely without punctuation, "The Escape" follows in the rich tradition of the innocent or naïve child narrator and tells of a childish adventure in which Sonia and René "run away." Perhaps an analogy for either a sexual exploit or an attempt to leave the island (a common if controversial theme), the story plays with language as it does with gender roles. The mixture of the narrator's journalistic objectivity interspersed with infrequent emotional comments by a first person narrator give "The Discovery" a unique feel. Apparently the story of a shipboard journey to an island colony of imperial Spain, this tale of gender relations and personal destiny offers two epiphanies and an open ending. The questions suggested by "It's in Me Somewhere" are more philosophical than religious in tone, and deal with the seedy traffic in flesh that was made illegal from the onset of the Revolution, but that has made a comeback in the last decade. Here, a mother tries to convince her daughter that the life of a prostitute is not necessarily a path to sexual and economic liberation. "For Men Only" is an ironic and irreverent look at intolerant views of homosexuality characterizing early post-Revolution Cuba. On the surface a conflation of the Yankee capitalist and the pervert, in reality the story portrays a gay subject who is authoring his own history in the midst of an atmosphere of secrecy and oppression. The teenage girl narrating "We Blacks All Drink Coffee" is full of youthful fervor and rebellion against the status quo. This tale offers a nostalgic recall of the author's experiences as a voluntary *brigadista,* picking coffee in a rural plantation. Rife with symbols of the revolution, including a verse from the Cuban hero José Martí and a title that juxtaposes race and the economy, the story explores the changing definition of Cuba as a nation. Narrated from the perspective of a little girl, "Havana Is a Really Big City" is a single paragraph that runs four pages, capturing the turmoil of political transition, economic shortages, and emotional havoc through the eyes of a child. Although the last scene in the story hints that it is situated directly before the revolution, images of the girl's crowded and crumbling house draw a clear correlation to contemporary Havana as well.

The "other tales" are taken mostly from the prize-winning 1988 book *El Diablo son las cosas,* whose title story is rendered here as "Go Figure." Debatably a negative commentary on men's perception of women, a young man narrates the antics of his neighbor, Miss Betty. In truth, the universally applicable theme of the story is the comedy of everyday life. In "The Beatles vs. Duran Duran" a middle-aged mother who was a *brigadista* has to jump the generation gap in order to learn a lesson about contemporary culture and revolution from her daughter. A similar protagonist narrates "Kid Bururú and the Cannibals." While taking a nostalgic trip through Havana to celebrate her fortieth birthday, she is confronted with the problematic issues of machismo and race relations in Cuba, which are supposed to have already been solved, and finds more revealed than she bargained for. In "Prophet of Doom," the narration is permeated with an erotic mysticism reflecting the cultural currency of the syncretic mixture of Catholicism and Afro-Cuban religions. Far from forgotten in the socialist country, religious ritual—complete with blessings and curses—regulates the sexual epiphany of the unwilling and skeptical protagonist. Another story of self-discovery, "The Blind Buffalo" follows the awakening of a young woman who discovers early that her imagination and magic (of words, of a talisman coin) will take her out of the small dusty town of Esmeralda. As a successful woman who has transcended small-town limitations, the final lesson she learns is about humility and love. "No Call of the Wild," the most recently written tale (2007), closes this collection with the somber tone of the first story, reflecting the desperation and anguish in Havana in the early new century. Clearly patterned after the Jack London classic, this tale of misplaced loyalty and betrayal invites interpretations on several levels.

PRINCIPAL WORKS IN SPANISH BY YÁÑEZ

Sangra por la herida (novel, 2010)
El búfalo ciego y otros cuentos (short stories, 2008)
Del azafrán al lirio (essays, 2006)
Falsos documentos (short stories, 2005)
Camila y Camila (essays, 2003)
Un solo bosque negro (poetry, 2003)
Cubanas a capítulo (essays, 2001)
Narraciones desordenadas e incompletas (short stories, 1997)
Algún lugar en ruinas (poetry, 1997)
El diablo son las cosas (short stories, 1988, 2001)
Las visitas y otros poemas (poetry, 1986)
La hora de los mameyes (novel, 1983)
La Habana es una ciudad bien grande (short stories, 1981)
Todos los negros tomamos café (short stories, 1976)
Las visitas (poetry, 1971)

HAVANA IS A REALLY BIG CITY

THE MOURNER

The pebbles on the road formed little bundles under his shoes. Hard tumors ruthlessly digging themselves into the soles of his feet. Occasionally, fruit would fall from the trees lining the path, and his feet would mash them with a soft plop. His foot would feel itself grinding the rose-colored pulp. So soft. And then the pebbles again.

This time a faint smell kept pace with him, a blend of petroleum, moist earth, and wood, so very peculiar. Only a month ago he had traveled this very same route. Back then, however, both sensations had eluded him. He had simply dragged his legs, such old legs, behind the hearse taking Matilde away. And what about the anguish he had felt? It had been like a pouch swelling and hardening inside his throat. Matilde would have known that on occasions such as those his mind would go blank. People say that pain renders the senses more acute, that it allows us to perceive the dew on the leaves, the fluttering of an insect's wings. "Maybe that's true with physical pain," Matilde would have said, "but the other sort just stupefies you, Severino. You don't know how to grieve about things like you should."

"I don't know how to mourn, Matilde. It's only after everything is over and done with that I feel as if someone were scraping the inside of my chest with sandpaper."

"It's obvious that you're a carpenter," Matilde answered. "I, for one, just plunge right into the pain from the very start. You don't know how to suffer."

But deep in her inner recesses, Matilde knew him well. No other woman had ever delved into the very core of his being like she had. Six months after the death of their son, Severino had broken down and begun sobbing like a child. On that day at noon, having come across a hastily scribbled note in their son's handwriting, the letters sloping on the paper as if rushing into life, Severino's sorrow had burst like a floodstream. His head on Matilde's lap, he had heard her asking him softly if the sandpaper had started to grind away at his heart.

When he had followed the hearse taking Matilde away, he had felt nothing, he had smelled nothing.

Now, on his first visit to her gravesite, the pebbles dug holes into his shoes, and the fruit—what did the fruit do to him? Past and present trampled across his chest in broad, sweeping strides. The two of them, so very young, naked, at Matilde's favorite hour, six, seven o'clock in the evening, twilight. Or at dawn, their eyes still throbbing with the final images of their dreams. Dreaming in color is a bad idea, Severino. Try to dream in black and white.

"I can't, Matilde. No matter how hard I try."

He wondered how Matilde was. He didn't believe in heaven anymore. But that other notion remained. The color of the body transformed by the effects of death. The smells. The maggots. It was best not to think about it. You never want to think about anything bad, Matilde used to tell him. She had told him the same thing for fifty years. It had been the first thing she'd said to him when they'd met on the third-class deck of the boat taking them to Cuba as immigrants. Piled on top of one another. The storm, the German submarine in sight, the boat in darkness, the end of life as they knew it, and Severino daringly slipping his hand down the lace of her neckline. Don't you ever think of anything bad? Severino, feeling the yielding flesh hardening under his fingers, had not replied. He had simply ruminated about how fucking hungry they were all going to be because of the war. Their son had been sent back to them from a dank prison cell in La Cabaña broken with tuberculosis, which is why Severino got the idea of taking their daughter for a stroll through Luna Park every afternoon. That had been thirty years earlier. During Matilde's death throes, he had spent his time mending his fingernails with a nickel-plated nail clipper. You never want to face anything bad.

"Comrade," the voice startled him. A young man was staring at him fixedly. Severino's thoughts reeled back. Now you're going to say the first idiotic thing that pops into your head, Matilde would have said. But who did this man think he was to butt into his thoughts like that?

"Comrades...like a couple of jackasses? What do you want?"

The man seemed to retreat. But without taking a step. As if from within.

"I'm very sorry, sir."

Severino heard the words as if they came from a great distance away. Like a scratch on a record.

"I didn't mean to disturb you," the young man continued. "I'm looking for the firemen's monument."

"The firemen's monument?" Severino examined the backs of his wrinkled hands. "Just one more block, on the sidewalk to your right."

"I appreciate it," the man said as farewell.

Severino felt abruptly alone. At the age of seventy-three, he had been left all alone. That is why he had become so preoccupied with smells, with reminiscences crowding ever more lightly into his consciousness, by the pebbles digging into his shoes and the fruit caressing the soles of his feet.

A hearse came up alongside him. Ah, Severino said to himself. Another one going heaven knows where. He lifted his gaze and glanced at the procession advancing in utter loneliness down the path. Not a single mourner. Not even a nosegay. Who can it be in the coffin? Someone who lived a long life, probably too long. At funerals, from afar, one can only guess whether it's an adult or a child. There's something heartrending and luminous about a small white coffin. But this one. A corpse with no mourners, whoever it was. Not a wife, not a single relative, not even a friend. No one to mourn him. This poor wretch is alone. Alone in death. Loneliness is for the fucking birds, Matilde."

"Hey, driver. The dead man's name..."

"Rodríguez."

"Ah."

The hearse rolled down an alley... Severino followed at his own pace, while he felt the sky darkening above him.

"It's going to rain," he remarked.

"No," said the chauffeur. "It's the sparrows."

Severino glanced sideways at the cloud of sparrows fluttering above the procession. We're not so alone anymore, Matilde. What a silly habit of engaging in silent conversation this is. No one to accompany Rodríguez on his last journey. The pebbles, the fruit, the sandpaper scraping the inside of his breast.

"You need a hand," he said to the chauffeur, a slight tone of inquiry in his voice.

The car had stopped by the side of two men in work clothes waiting before a grave ready for a burial. Between the four of them they carefully slid the coffin onto long, broad leather strips.

"I'm very sorry, my friend," the voice of one of the gravediggers was nasal, sorrowful. Severino ran his hand over his eyes. Crying. What a spectacle, he thought.

"Are you the chief mourner?" the chauffeur asked.

Severino shrugged his shoulders and didn't reply. He paused a moment longer to leave for Rodríguez the flowers he had bought thinking of Matilde. She would have understood right away. She would have sympathized with that gesture in honor of comrade Rodríguez, who had almost had to travel alone in death. Loneliness is for the fucking birds. Matilde.

Translated by Lizbeth Paravisini-Gebert

THE ESCAPE

I'm nine years old and my name is Sonia   in the mornings I go to school and in the afternoons I go outside to play with René mommy doesn't want me to play with René but I tell her that what I like is for her to let me go down to the street because you can't talk with dolls like I do with René who is my friend René talks a lot and he knows a bunch of good games   he is teaching me to tie my hands behind my back and then how to untie them and how to keep a little frog in my pocket without hurting it   René is nine just like me but he's smaller and skinnier   and if we stand next to each other he always tries to cheat so he'll seem as tall as I am but I always win and René gets mad and says that some day I'm going to wake up shrunken and he'll be big   as big as a giant and then I'll be really afraid of him   and that René is going to put me inside his hat and he's going to lift me up very high very high very high so that I can see what's on the other side of that little line where the ocean ends and that's how it happened   that I wanted to see and I wanted to walk around   that we should leave without mommy finding out and that René should take me to look for treasure and to go around alone without daddy and mommy and to get lost in the woods or in a gully or something like that   but that everybody would think that we had died and so one day we would return when we were big and René had a beard probably and then that we would talk all funny so that no one could understand   only René and I would understand us   I wanted all that but René told me that I was going to be afraid to run away from home and that since I'm a little girl then I was going to start crying and wanting to go home again with my mommy   but I told him no no no   that I wasn't going to cry and since we had like eighty cents that René had got and I think that with that you can go really far we began to plan the trip in secret   without telling anyone and we left one afternoon so that we wouldn't miss school that day and

I brought crackers for the road and daddy's yellow cap in case it was cold and René also brought a black jacket from when his grandfather was a sailor and in a paper bag the snack that he had saved from the morning some bananas   and the eighty cents   and I think that when he came to get me he was a little bit afraid even though he didn't want to admit it   I already knew that René didn't want to leave and that he was going to miss his mom and his grandmother a lot and then I told him that my poor mommy when she was left without me   and it was at that moment that he started crying while we were walking along and seeing for the last time all the pretty things on our street   the broken curb on the sidewalk where the water flows like a waterfall when it rains a lot the big lock on the railing that who knows why never gets opened   the little flower that grows between the bricks and that we always think is about to die or to be completely swallowed up by the bricks   but René didn't say even once that we should stay   and I didn't say anything either even though I am a little girl   and when we passed by our school René stopped crying and started laughing and I also thought it was very funny to be thinking what René was probably thinking and that was what a look the teacher would have on her face when she found out about everything   that René and I had left   run away   and that we were passing in front of the school and no one knew anything   and that now only René and I knew it   and René then took the package of crackers and carried it for me and I put daddy's yellow cap on him so that he would look more like a pirate with his grandfather's black jacket   and then René took my hand and gave me his silver pocket knife   René's pretty knife that I've wanted him to lend me forever   and he never had done it   and now I was so happy that I could no longer remember mommy or anything else and I only was thinking that René and I were leaving together and that I finally had René's silver knife   that René was a pirate with the yellow cap and the eighty cents in his grandfather's jacket and suddenly René said that we had arrived and it was the sea wall   we sat there to eat the crackers and we saved the bananas for later   and we began to wait for a boat to pass so we could stow away in its hold because we were two pirates who were escaping from a very big, very old castle that was full of spiders and had a hunchback who rang the bells at night   and the people passed by without realizing that René and I were two very evil pirates and that we were going to do away with all of them when we finished eating the crackers   and René covered his eyes with the cap and laughed a lot every time that the ocean sprayed us   and with the tip of my knife I wrote in the wall and I put **Sonia**   and then I put **and René**   and it was very sunny and René kept laughing and I felt like yelling René René René and that was when daddy arrived and began to shout and to spank me   and he pulled me off the wall grabbing me hard by the arm   and I was kicking him and telling him that I was a pirate who was going to escape   and René said that he was going to cut his head off with the silver knife if he didn't let me go but daddy didn't pay any attention to him and while he was dragging me I looked back crying and I saw René standing in front of the wall looking at me   with the yellow cap in his hand and the eighty cents in his grandfather's jacket.

Translated by Victoria L. McCard

THE DISCOVERY

The press of that era reveals what occurred. The steamer had disembarked from the metropolis various weeks prior on its way to the populous village of Saint Christopher of Havana. After navigating drizzle and currents in no great hurry, it faced its destiny right on the coast of that city.

The vessel was overloaded. It was the custom of the shipping lines to pay for the trip by packing in like sardines rustic Spaniards of lesser means who, living on top of each other throughout the journey and staying alive on rancid cheese, sighed in anticipation of promised riches, utopian mines transformed with the passing years into *bodegas,* ironworks, and hardware shops. Well-heeled families made the passage in private, albeit uncomfortable, berths that did not escape the pestilent proximity to various critters picked up at stops at previous ports.

These families came out once in a while to enjoy the fresh air and rub elbows with the Admiral and the troops that accompanied him in his venture to discover a New World. Each one of them, in their own way, was on a mission to conquer. Craftsmen specializing in espadrille and haversacks, youths on fire for French ideals, young bucks who avidly exchanged glances with voluptuous and well-endowed savages, all bounced their way through the Gulf of Mexico, mimicking the gesture of the lighthouse watchman.

In one of those berths traveled a Castilian family. Husband and wife, two children, and a poor relative that functioned as a servant.

Dragged along by the rumors of instantaneous fortunes, Ramiro had thrown himself into the adventure of crossing the ocean with all of his worldly possessions.

Antonia was one of those possessions. Daughter of a ruined aristocrat, destined for the convent, she was rescued from her father's house by that man with starch-stiff moustache, a prosperous businessman that brought her back to life and gave her two sons.

During the first ten years of their marriage the couple's life had rolled along smoothly. At the table, as well as in bed, Antonia made tremendous displays of attention and delicacy, mused Ramiro. I could wish for nothing more. And I return her affection with plenty of enthusiasm. Enthusiasm that she parceled out competently between her chores and their moments of intimacy.

Ramiro was an even-tempered man. And he had let himself go off the deep end over the idea of setting himself up in the new territories. Ah, over there, where those who set off to never return, and if they do they come back with such stories and memories, Antonia, that I just can't be satisfied unless I try my luck.

The preparations took quite some time. From the moment the seed of that formidable move had been sown in the family's imagination, until the exact instant they were underway from the Canary Islands, passed two interminable years, during which the home's tranquility was turned upside down by transactions, packing, and good-byes.

The old marquis, robbed of his grandsons, didn't let a day go by without offering one more tragic prediction. "Disasters will befall you: mysterious fevers, fish that gobble you up down to your bones, encounters with cannibals." In bitter disputes with his son-in-law, he reproached him for his stubbornness. Antonia spoke not a word about the voyage. She was resigned due to the obstinacy of her husband, and apprehensive, on the other hand, because of her father's melancholy. Antonia spent her afternoons in the church or her bedroom, wrapped up in herself. I would follow my husband even if he insisted on going to the ends of the earth and throwing himself off headfirst, she thought.

But as their exodus grew nearer, and particularly from the precise day on which they arrived with the carriages to their point of departure, Antonia slowly began to undergo a change. Looking at her sideways, one noted a certain joyful spark, something like what she had back in the first days of her marriage, when at the mere mention of her evaded destiny as a nun the hairs on the back of her neck would stand up in pure happiness and desire, as if the memory of her former virginity increased her pleasure at her new circumstances.

And I didn't know exactly what was happening to her, until the moment we weighed anchor, when I discovered her at one end of the ship with her eyes fixed on the sea. I spoke to her, I grabbed her arm, I pointed out her father falling apart sobbing against the pier, but it was all useless.

Antonia was being taken over by a sensation she had never felt before. Over the thirty-five years of her life she had been surrounded by arid buttes, dark foliage, dry stone barricades. Seeing the sea for the first time was beyond any comparison to what she had been told. It was as if a new woman was breaking out from underneath her very skin. She ended up associating it with her wedding night, when she could feel that, beneath the profound feeling of delight and surprise, a sharp yet enduring ache had set in. That was what the sea was like.

In a stupor, Ramiro began to comprehend, in the most rudimentary way, that little by little he was gaining a rival. Of that docile woman with whom he had shared ten years of his life, not a single sign remained. Antonia kept abandoning him to run out on the deck and contemplate the horizon with a glazed look in her eyes. Her sons were left to the care of her cousin, who busied herself with keeping them clean and feeding them, and who as default took care of Antonia's husband with a kindness that gave Ramiro anguished memories of the peaceful days from before.

The crossing was long and full of privations in those times. It was necessary to spend days at a time without leaving one's berth in order to stop feeling so seasick, to escape feeling beaten by the waves. The man had a difficult time of it keeping Antonia confined. An overriding force would propel her outside, and without directing a word to anyone, nor listening to a bit of advice, she would lean her elbows on the railing, where she would stay for hours and hours regardless of whether it was night or day.

When at the end of several weeks land was spotted, a wave of tranquility invaded Ramiro's soul. The thought that his marriage would be able to return to how it was before comforted him. I am just torn apart by the idea that there is no living creature on whom I can focus this jealousy, a jealousy that is roasting me alive from the inside out, he thought. Strange maneuverings crossed his mind, schemes of how to get his wife away from that devastating influence. He changed their plans of settling in the capital; built a castle in the air that would be encircled by mountains, imitating the way of life in their native land; and finally determined to shower Antonia with attention. May it make her forget forever this itinerary that has been so ruinous for our lives.

One morning, the first thing spied by the eyes of the emigrants was the spiky silhouette of the eastern mountains. The vessel made its entry slowly into the port of Santiago de Cuba, the last stop before arriving to Havana.

Only two people left the ship. One of them was a sharp-eyed lad, who no sooner had glimpsed land than he jumped over the cables like a rat; the other was the husband, who stirred to action by his decision to get things settled as soon as possible in the island's interior, decided to disembark in Santiago to take care of the necessary business quickly, while the ship made its way toward the capital. Because of my eagerness to recover my wife, my Antonia.

Luck turned against him in a curious way.

The steamship continued along its route. Even as it became harder and harder to see clearly through the distance, Ramiro was able to make out Antonia's rapt gaze, which far from the mountains and the coast lost itself in the sea.

The rest is a matter of public record. The husband made the rest of the journey over land, fighting tooth and nail against time to get to the pier and welcome his family. He arrived to the city in the middle of a heavy windstorm, and his only thought was for the ship that should have made its landing that very afternoon in the Havana port. The first news that reached him was that the vessel had attempted entry that morning, but the strong winds prevented its coming into the bay. The second installment, which I lived in the wee hours of the next morning was the onset of such a tropical storm as hadn't been seen in ages by the town's inhabitants—woe to those on the ship. He sensed the third strike as if in a dream, and it pierced his heart: the ocean liner would be swallowed by the waves. And with it his sons, his fortune, and his wife.

He ran to the seawall, which like a belt of stone bordered the port, and tried to make out, through the dawn fog, the familiar lines of the vessel. But that too was all in vain. As were all of the attempts in the following days to find the boat, or at the very least the flotsam and jetsam from the disaster; whether on the part of Ramiro or of the island's government, they had no results whatsoever. The ship had been lost forever.

Nobody ever found out what happened, nor what had transpired in those final moments of the tragic contingent that had remained aboard. It was never known whether in truth the ship had gone down. In those years old stories would circulate about phantom vessels that continued to cruise for centuries, driven by who knows what mysterious forces. At any rate, it was not difficult to imagine Antonia leaning on the guardrail, full of anticipation, her heart captured by love for the first time, never to set her foot on solid ground again.

Translated by Sara E. Cooper

IT'S IN ME SOMEWHERE

You know I still remember, and it still makes my blood boil. What I've had to go through, there are no words to describe it. I wouldn't go back to that life over my dead body. And don't start saying I'm indoctrinating you. Oh, please. What it is, I've been around the block once or twice. And I could tell you all about it from A to Z. Any one of those little stories that are hidden away in some corner of my mind, and no matter how much I try to forget, they come out and take a little walk from time to time. I'm going to have to bring out the smelling salts when I get finished talking. But all that aside. Because there are things in life that, when they happen, you decide that it's better to keep them under your hat and quiet-like, rather than spreading them all around and bringing everybody else down. Who hasn't gone through something that they have hauled along with them all through the years and would rather be hit by a train than tell anybody about it. So I don't know how you are dragging it all out of me. But you just told me that you are leaving the country, and you're going to become a whore, and that I, who was one until just recently, like they say, I want to put on the airs of a goody-two-shoes. All of that with your tongue looser than a caboose. So I'm going to tell you, even if afterward I have to take you to the emergency room. In the beginning I wasn't someone who had to eat crumbs with the dregs of society. I was right up there, believe me. My daddy, may he rest in peace, although I believe he died all twisted up on account of what he was leaving behind, and he must have stayed turned around in disgust for a good long while, he showed me how to read and write, with very nice penmanship in Palmer calligraphy, and before the family had that run of bad luck with the old man's illness and the death of my brother Quique up in the U.S., I was quite the little lady of the house, I even mangled a little English, and of course I had my drop of *carabalí*². So in the skin trade I started off passing for a fine piece of merchandise, because I was a classy girl. Not for just any old guy. And as one soon acquires a thick skin in that line of work, I even felt I was better than the girls who walked the streets, when I went regularly to a clean, orderly place where they treated me like a queen. And when a *gentleman* arrived, I already knew he was mine. I would even sometimes come home with a new word of English that I had learned and I would say it over and over without knowing what it meant. My old man would get so sore he'd turn purple there on the couch because he had been a waiter in Texas and he knew a thing or two himself. Many times they'd be so upset they were eating with the money I brought home, I would have to pat the old man's head and play up to Mama so she wouldn't cry, and say that better days were coming. Better days. What a crock. I still remember what happened and I don't know whether to cry or what. Bad luck, when it rains it pours. First it was my brother Quique: from one day to the next a letter showed up saying to Mama, "Shit, I'm dying," and then a card from who knows who, to let us know he was six feet under in a city I can't even remember its name. Then Daddy gets sick and loses his job, Mama has a bad heart and I get started with that new business. At least we had enough to keep going, pay for our room in the tenements and eat on a daily basis. Then one day it all came down. Every little bit of it. The police came and had it out with Obdulia, the owner of the whorehouse. Damn assassins: Sundays they'd be out strolling with their wives in tow, and when they were on shift in the squad car they'd rob us without blinking an eye, and if Ms. Obdulia didn't pay them off on time, then there really was hell to pay. To make a long story short, the same day I lost my job and my old man, because when I got home with the bad news, I didn't even have to report it, because I ran into Mama with her arms around Papa who had just gone out like a light and died with his coffee cup in his hand.

---

² *El que no tiene de congo tiene de carabalí.* (If you don't have any Congo, you have Carabalí.) Popular Cuban saying that refers to two African tribes, implying that every Cuban has a bit of African blood.

And without spilling a drop, ladies and gentlemen. The last few bucks went for the wake and in dressing the old man in a decent suit of clothes, although with him getting all twisted up it took a hell of an effort to get the *guayabera* on him, and it never did look quite right. But we did it right and Mama was happy. Inside I was saying to myself, "Virgencita, what do I do now?" I didn't have any choice but to start hoofing it out on the street and get to know what it was to wait and hope, through rain or cold, for a client to appear. Whoever. Anybody. But I put on airs and didn't get a thing. I came back to the flat dead broke, and Mama looking at me with the face of a sacrificial lamb, because we hadn't had a hot meal in a week. We tried to make do with the fritters sold at the stand on the corner. And that was with me going hungry, not a bite, for three whole days; I'd buy Mama a fried pie and would give her the story that I had already eaten mine on the way. What torture that was. The half a block I had to walk from that stand to our building, I would stare at that fritter and tell myself that she wouldn't notice just a nibble, and if she did, I could tell her they sold it to me like that. I would touch the edges, pull off a minute piece or two, put them in my mouth. Then it felt worse. I would get back to the room ready to eat a horse if it was put in front of me. And I would give Mama the twenty-millionth fritter, and I would go wash my hands in the washbasin, because just catching a whiff of the grease would start my stomach turning and I would feel like I was going to faint right then and there. So I would go out to work every single night, even though it was hurricane season, when there were so few people on the streets that I didn't know how long we would have to be hungry. The eighth night was when that old lady, dressed to the nines, parked her Plymouth on the corner where I was strutting, stuck her head out of the window and looked me up and down. I told myself, "Oh, just what I needed," and I turned around and acted like I was looking at the mannequins in the store display on Virtues St., to see whether that old crone would get the hell out of there. But who would believe that after a little while I turn half-way around and there I am with that woman, who has to be at least eighty, wearing a ton of gold, her head cocked to one side, looking at me like I was a monkey in a zoo. "It's for my son," she said, just like that, as if she wanted to close the deal quickly. I kept quiet, to tell the truth, because I didn't know what to say. And without anything else, she pulled me over slowly to the Plymouth. I got in without thinking about it much, or rather, I was thinking about what I was going to do with all the money I earned. Because although it was very strange that a lady of the upper crust would be looking for someone like me for her son at eleven o'clock at night, it's also just a fact that at the crossroads of one's life, the gears can turn a little slowly, and I couldn't get my mind off of the smorgasbord there would be the next day. So I told the ancient lady, "Okay," and I went off with the old bag. At first she wouldn't even glance at me, but after a bit she took out a bill and looked me right in the eyes. Like sizing me up. To me it seemed there wasn't anything obvious in the way that she told me, "twenty now and twenty *afterward*," just like in the American movies when they send the gangster off on a mission impossible. I don't know if it was the way that she said *afterward*, or the amount she was offering, which in those days was enough to make you feel like a millionaire. What happened was that I got a knot in my throat, but I told myself not to be such a sissy and to take advantage of my good luck, that a chance like this was a once in a lifetime deal. My mind was playing that game of tug of war when the Plymouth pulled through a gate covered in ice plants, that made me think we were in Miramar. Afterward you better believed I looked for it. But nothing. Sometimes I run into it up on the Hill and say to myself, "That's it!" But it isn't. Or I'll be walking through Vedado and I'll think, surprised, "Here, now I've found it." But I'm wrong again. Another gate like that one, with the ice plants sharpening their spikes through the bars, doesn't exist. It's like the earth swallowed it up. But if in that moment when the old lady parked the car and told me to go in without a peep so the servants didn't wake up, if I had pinched myself hard to see if I was having a nightmare, I would have left a trail of black blood, that's how scared I was. And we passed through a kitchen that was five times bigger than our room at home, and there on top of the table somebody had left a covered crystal platter full of chicken and rice, and my eyes went right to it, so that even the old lady noticed and repeated to me, *"Afterward."* And when I heard her say that again, was when I saw that in my hand I held a twenty-dollar bill, smooth, smelling delicious, a bill like I hadn't seen in a very long time. Then I put it away and said to myself that it was all downhill from there, no matter what happened. As if. It felt like I had a thorn piercing me. Because as we were climbing the stairs, I sensed that the old lady wanted to tell me something, and it made me so mad I said, "Spill it." She gave me a look and I felt like a rag you use to wash the floor. But she didn't answer me. That was when I started looking around to see where I'd have to run to get out if the situation got too hairy. At that we came up to a half-shut door, and there the old lady spoke to me. Her words engraved themselves onto my brain, I'll still remember in my grave. Like I was a stray dog, she told me, "Behave yourself, my son is very special." *Very special.* It still comes back to me and makes my blood boil, so I feel like I'm going to go off like a firecracker. I walked into the room and what did I find there? In the bed was a kind of sickly white creature, covered up to its chest with a sheet. Unshaven. At first glance I couldn't see exactly what the problem was, but then when I saw him move his paws, how he slobbered, the noises he made in his throat, I shrilled, "But ma'am, this is a monster!" She gave me a hard stare, her eyes sharp as fangs, and answered, "I'm paying." And I remembered that new twenty, the other twenty waiting for me, Mama and her bad heart in our room, and the three months of back rent we owed. Even the chicken and rice wormed its way into my thoughts in that moment, because now all the pistons were firing for sure. And behind my eyelids I saw the crystal platter growing and growing, swelling like a balloon in the kitchen, and the rice spilling out from the cover; the radio announcer in the middle of our tenement room, the tenement room overflowing with chicken and rice and that jingle Jon Chi Rice, Chi's so fluffy, Chi's never sticky, You're gonna love Chi. And I stared at that fat thing and felt the knot in my throat again, and this time it was churning up and down from my belly to my throat and back again. And with all of that I told the old lady that everything was fine, that I was going to find it in me somewhere. And when the old bag was going to leave the room, that knot that was passing through my chest must have hit my heart. And I fell flat on the floor. I guess that it created a huge scene in the house, because the old lady thought that I had died. And I think I did, that I died a little bit. And when I came to in the Plymouth, the guy driving said that he was the chauffeur, that everybody in the whole house had woken up with all the racket, and that the boss lady told him to tell me to forget about everything and to keep the twenty bucks as long as I didn't open my mouth. For him to take me to the hospital. And I said, "Hospital my ass, I don't see anybody dying here." And for him to just please drop me off at the next corner, and I got out of the Plymouth like a bat out of hell. But why are you making that kind of face? I suppose you think your own mother is going to lie to you. Don't stare at me like that, you look like you're going to have a stroke.

Translated by Sara E. Cooper

FOR MEN ONLY

Although in more than one occasion that phrase had appeared scrawled on the doors to the men's restrooms, it didn't mean that in the offices of the placid bank on Galiano Street there was some sort of conspiracy brewing against the powers that be. Nothing of the sort.

Everyone could reread it at his leisure: *mister Morris maricón*—"flaming faggot."

If you really thought about it, it wasn't the first time that the company's employees manifested, in one way or another, their discontent with authority, whether it be in veiled inefficiency in operations, or in shadily wasteful maneuvers that little by little undermined the command and decisions of the director. On the other hand, nevertheless, no one could say whether or not said *mister* Morris had earned the nickname that just wouldn't disappear from the urinals.

It almost seemed demonic. When you least expected it, the sign was back again.

Each time the same scene went down in the offices. Some functionary or another would spread the news, the rumor flew until reaching the Vice-President's ears, he would come out of his office violently loosening the knot of his tie, he would go into the men's room and within seconds he would be coming back, slamming door after slamming door, toward the private office of the director, *mister* Morris.

"What nerve, goddammit, and no less than here, at the National City Bank of New York! Of New York!!!" He pronounced the *w* with too much of a *u* sound, revealing that he had gone to school on the island. "And every single one of you are going to pay for this!"

And what was even more shocking was that it could happen at any hour of the day or night. On one occasion, when for entirely understandable reasons the night watchman had to leave his post around four o'clock in the morning, following the trail of his flashlight he noticed the door ajar and his eyes fell upon the impertinent declaration that had been scribbled pell-mell.

"Turn up the heat!" said the Vice-President.

They tried every method imaginable. At first it would be erased discretely, later you heard vague criticisms being passed along, and after that, blatant threats. They even ended up painting the doors some dark color, kind of a brown, to thwart the guilty party's enterprise. But nothing worked; the announcement kept on turning up regularly.

When the insanity erupted, the board of directors called a general council in which the Vice-President—in front of the person in question, *mister* Morris himself—begged for prudence in appreciation of the good salary that the National City Bank of New York generously paid every two weeks and that the employees collected from his office. *Mister* Morris, during the entire meeting, did nothing but look from side to side, eyes fierce, without saying a word.

The signs continued.

The Vice-President's last resort was to yank the doors right out. Two or three days went by in apparent confusion, then one morning the audacity reached an incomprehensible high: the insult showed up on the very door of *mister* Morris's private suite. This time accompanied by drawings alluding to the topic.

In those days the city was all in a flutter. Coming into the 1930s, the whole island was busy in one riotous enterprise or another. The repressive body of the State didn't have the resources to defend the bruised honor of *mister* Morris, even if he was the poster child of the U.S.

Stories recounting the tribulations of the director of the Galiano Street Bank even reached the ears of the very President of the Constitutional Republic.

"Let him bugger somewhere else," was the response of the petty tyrant, who was already too caught up in the headaches brought on at every turn by the national revolt. But the United States Embassy butted in, and the Secret Service was obliged to intervene under strict orders of the President, who was obliged to take care of the matter so he wouldn't have to deal with—in addition to internal problems—an external offensive from the Global Power just because of *mister* Morris's wounded dignity. "This is not the moment to stir up the marines, just on account of some screwing around here or there," he concluded.

An investigation was opened. One day at lunchtime, three Secret Service agents made their grand entrance into the bank, accompanied by bodyguards armed to the teeth. Along with them came an invasion of technicians who took fingerprints, reviewed all the files, made measurements, snapped photos of the scene of the crime, rummaged through the legal precedents, and one by one interrogated each and every employee under a spotlight. And they were buried in these tasks for various weeks, with no results whatsoever.

What most disconcerted the police was that they had never before encountered such a case. The Secret Service knew how to harass the unions, how to repress student protests, and how to use their nightstick on the more uncooperative workers. But protecting a faggot had never been a part of their job description. For that reason, if you can believe it, the viciousness that was unleashed was even worse than anyone could have expected.

"I want him here," said the Vice-President, as he pointed grimly with his index finger to the carpet of his office. "I want my scapegoat right here."

The Secret Service agent had strict orders: make the bank's board of directors happy. Hence, when in the midst of the investigation the proclamation of *mister* Morris's hidden frailties popped up yet again, written with chalk across the mirrors in the men's room, the brutality of the Machado regime fell upon the peaceful bank.

There were detentions in the wee hours of the morning; the employees suffered new interrogations, this time the questions coming complemented by fists and nightsticks; all the pens, pencils, and paintbrushes were confiscated; the boxes of chalk were warehoused and padlocked; and the bathrooms—they were roped in by a tight cordon of guards who, shoulder to shoulder, supervised each visitor to the toilets.

They were in this state of siege for a few days, until what had to happen, did. They found someone to blame.

Only a few months before the appearance of the signs, a new cashier had started, a slight man with a somewhat anemic countenance and good manners. He had kept himself distanced and silent during these weeks of delirium, as if all of it were happening somewhere else, and not under his very own nose. Also working at the bank—as a secretary—was a young lady of thirty-something long lost years. This Maria Isabel was his downfall. By who knows what strange phenomenon, the young lady was enraptured by her office mate with the insipid gaze, and tried to seduce him by every means at her disposal. No one knows whether or not he ever fathomed the dark passion that he had awakened in the secretary, or whether a congenital timidity had blocked his powers of observation as well as his eyesight, preventing him from perceiving the fiery glances that Maria Isabel shot at him every time they crossed paths.

What was obvious was that the young lady felt scorned and turned on him like a viper. Love was the motive, but Maria Isabel ended up being the instrument, the definitive lethal weapon. The first strike against the cashier annihilated him.

Although nobody had witnessed the private conversation that the secretary had with the Secret Service agents, it was easy to guess what she had said. She had noticed bits of black paint underneath the cashier's fingernails, fragments of chalk in the accounts office. Or even better, she had been passing by the door of the men's restroom and there he was, with his insipid gaze, his upraised hand tracing the last line of a newly painted sign: *mister Morris maricón.*

For the officials who were anxious to elude any further embarrassment connected to this sordid affair, the most insignificant indictment would have been enough. The Secret Service fell upon the little man like mangy vultures on road kill.

And so that the accusation would be even more conclusive, he was charged with as many crimes as they could think up: embezzlement, bribery, treason, and insulting a foreign government. He was subjected to beatings and torture and finally was condemned to forced labor in the Presidio Modelo.

What the poor clerk never found out was that, only two months after his incarceration, the Vice-President opened the door of his office at an unexpected hour and almost literally ran into the American, in the exact moment that he was writing across the expanse of the door, with great big satisfied letters, *mister Morris maricón*.

Translated by Sara E. Cooper

WE BLACKS ALL DRINK COFFEE

> *Tell me with what flowers*
> *you greased your plough*
> *so the fragrant land*
> *smells of spikenard?*
>
> José Martí

She says that I don't even know how to wash my own clothes and yet I want to go off. What is a mother's child going to do in a place like that? Just imagine what my grandmother would say if she knew, if she were to rise from the grave and see what the apple of her eye wanted to get into. It's a good thing she is dead, because if she weren't... There's a lot of talk about irresponsible mothers. But not about her.

And so my mother goes grumbling on and on from the end of the corridor where she has gone to take refuge so that her voice will be lost, will slip in between the furniture, so that the neighbors will not hear one word sounding louder than another, what would they think of this family, of this child of fifteen wanting to go off to pick coffee?

Things were different in her time. What would a well-brought-up girl be doing in the middle of the bush? Who would have thought of such a thing? Going where there are so many dangers. At least that's what the books say. Right into the heart of a titanic forest, a girl from a good family. Luckily there are no wild animals in this country.

For my mother the only safe place is my room with its four walls, a roof, a floor of the most ordinary sort. And not even then is it completely worthy of her confidence.

What do I care about the neighbors? But she does. And she closes the windows so that the argument will not go beyond this castle which is the protective shell of my family life. And when the room is the way she would have it, like the cell of a cloistered nun, she rushes forward from the other side of the corridor, she claps her hands. She shouts carefully. I am what is known as a girl who was given everything she ever wanted. If I asked for a flying bird, a flying bird I would get. Now look how ungrateful I was.

She says I think of no one but myself. I don't think of anyone, she says. One of my grandmothers is in the grave. If I insist on going off I'll be sending the other one to the edge of the grave. With a sudden collapse. All the catastrophes that could occur because of my pigheadedness. As the eldest, who has led a very sheltered life I should accept my responsibilities. The blood pressure of grandmothers and aunts can fall precipitously because of a *brigadista* who picks coffee.

There are so many dangers out in the country. No, my mother does not have a list on hand. A paper which she could unfurl from her chest like a banner, a string of unfamiliar words, the first of which would be disease. Who is going to look after you? When something goes wrong with your lungs. I am the one, she is the one, who will be responsible for you. A daughter at death's door for the rest of her life, kept in a room with all the windows closed to keep the early morning dew from coming in and the reproaches from going out, a daughter without any vital signs, without a will of her own, how wonderful. Withering away like a flower, filled with remorse to her last gasp for the folly of her adolescence. A trip to the coffee fields, and then a heroine dependent on the charity of a self-denying mother, always at her post with a load of comments such as 'it happened just as I warned you,' 'listen when you're told, or you'll never grow old,' 'that's what you get for disobeying your mother who wants the best for you,' for ever and ever. What more could she want?

In the mountains where they pick coffee, or so she has heard, she has never seen it with her own eyes—eyes the worms will soon be picking at thanks to all this heartbreak—the mountains are slippery and treacherous. They slip from under the feet and leave the *brigadistas* hanging in mid-air, from a branch. The plants of the red and green coffee beans are like waves sweeping over a little girl of fifteen who knows nothing of life.

And if afterwards her period, her menstruation, is one, two months late, what will the family think of this child who has risked losing her honor going to do voluntary work? For though it is not actually said, honor is not something you can touch, or see, it is only something you lose. And where will they look for her, where will they go, where would they complain? She will not be the first to have left home a good little girl and to have returned, at best, pregnant. And then, how awful it would be. The whole family having turned its back on her; the neighbors reveling in the gossip; the little girl the talk of the town.

What argument can counter this? How can I know in August if my period will be right on time in October, in December and in all the months to come? What guarantee can I give my mother that I will safeguard the family's precious honor? What a strange agreement to have to sign just to go pick coffee. Breaking my back at work for forty-five days, and still having to make sure that all my functions are in place with every gland responding on time. No defect in my body to provoke the anger of such a decent family as mine. Having to contend with the suspicious glances of my mother's fearsome neighbors. What a way to screw up someone's life, I tell myself.

And who knows if the coffee-picking mightn't turn your head so much that you even fall in love with a Negro, she says in a powerless rage.

You know what it means to be a nice white girl. As white as the paper daisy that my mother is crushing nervously between her hands in my birthday photograph, its yellow heart overflowing with innocence. For a white girl must receive maximum care, must be brought up according to all the rules of good health, and hygiene. She cannot go alone out onto the street. She must go with her father to the movies. She goes to school holding her mother's hand. She must not play with others. And never, never get into mischief.

How times change.

You are, I am, she says, the ones who stand to lose. If my mother would only let me explain to her. If only there were some way of getting out of her head those visions which she is hurling at me from every corner of the room, as she moves about, her voice louder and fiercer with every minute. In this room of white people living together as a family. Where the ancestors have most certainly been white. Where I tell her, who knows what kind of blood anyone has? That in the mother country, there had been dark-skinned Moors for centuries, no-one can avoid it. That those who do not have the Congo in them somewhere...[3]

My mother raises her hands to her bosom so as not to hear me, so as not to let another sentence in. So as to separate me from her breath. So as not to listen to me saying I am not a white paper daisy which she keeps between perfumed handkerchiefs. What is the point? What if I fall in love with a Negro? This is important, I learn for the first time in my life. The colors, shades, the tones of voice which show me for what I am within these four walls, in the bush I am going to, or on the street corner, this little lily-white girl, carefully watching a man with his fly shamelessly open.

Still clasping her breast, my mother retreats along the corridor, saying, 'do as you think best.'

Translated by Claudette Williams

---

[3] *El que no tiene de congo tiene de carabalí.* (If you don't have any Congo, you have Carabalí.) Popular Cuban saying that refers to two African tribes, implying that every Cuban has a bit of African blood.

HAVANA IS A REALLY BIG CITY

Havana is a really big city. That's what my mother says, and she knows a lot about these things. They say that a child can get lost in it forever. That two people can be looking for each other for years and never meet. But I like my city. Even though some day I might be alone and never again find my house or my friends. When I get big I'm going to make a map so I won't get lost. It must be really sad to get lost in a city. That's why I never go very far from my house. My house is one of those that is falling down it's so old. It's full of corners to hide in and wherever you are you can hear the noise from the street. I really like to go down there and look for bugs in the puddle that forms around the drain at the corner where the sidewalk caves in and the water pools up for months, or scrape the bricks on the wall with my penknife and discover the ants' hiding places, or exchange trading cards with the other children. But my mom won't let me go down to the street anymore. She says that it's dangerous and so I spend the days shut up in my house, without going out. My house is long like a lizard and all the rooms are connected to each other. To separate my room from hers, Grandmother moved over a sideboard. Between the sideboard and the wall there is a kind of cave where I have my toys and where I play explorer, or general, or doctor. Before my dad left, he also played there with me, behind the sideboard. Now he's not here and my mother listens to the radio at night, hidden under a bedspread so that no one will hear her, and she tells me that it's dangerous to go down to the street. If my dad returns some day from wherever he is the three of us will be able to go out like before. And we'll have money to paint the house which looks like it's about to crumble to pieces. The walls of the living room are peeling and I like to pull off little pieces of plaster and form figures like elephants, ships, and lions. I love animals a lot but my grandmother doesn't. It bothers her to see the walls without paint. That's why I can only tear up the walls when Grandmother goes out to take a walk or to run some errands, and I'm alone with my mom who doesn't care about the white patches anymore and who is even happy if the elephant really looks like an elephant. When she gets home, Grandmother gets so mad that it seems like she wants to bite our heads off, but she doesn't bite anyone because my mom always defends me. Poor little thing, he's alone all day, what do you expect the child to do if he gets bored, he's really pretty good, shut up in the house all the time. They don't let me go out to play and I'm already anxious for winter vacation to end so I can go back to school. The school is also crumbling from age. The desks are so full of scratches, names, and drawings, that it seems like there's not room for even one more. And yet a new one always appears on top of the others, covering them for a while until still another drawing, name, or a sharper penknife arrives. The posters on the walls are so faded that you can barely tell that the pink stain was once a great flock of flamingos, and the blue stain a big blue fish with its mouth open. Even so all the children know by heart that the pink stain was a flock of flamingos before, and the blue stain a big blue fish, and we talk about them as the flamingos and the blue fish, and everybody knows that we are referring to the faded posters that are hanging on the left-hand wall of the classroom. On the right-hand wall are the windows. Three windows. Two open and one closed, because if you open that window the sun shines in the teacher's face. The two open windows look out on the school patio, and when we get no recess, punishment for having talked in class or for something else, like when Sixth B began to sing *jingle bell, here comes Fidel,* and we sang with them, and the teacher got really nervous and the principal said that she was going to put all of them and us in jail, without really knowing why, we began to shout *strike, strike, strike,* and we didn't get recess for a week, we could see the other children running around and throwing balls made of paper and empty cigarette packs that had been cut into strips. And you get itchy feet and you want to run outside too. We would all like for those two windows to be closed like the one where the sun shines on the teacher's face. Against the wall in front are the teacher's desk and the blackboard. In the back there's a closet where the jars of white paste are kept. Some of them have the brush inside and if you take out the brush with the top they're always covered with paste and you get your fingers stuck together. There are also many sheets of colored paper for art and the chalk and the reading books. That closet is never open. Classes end at four. At that time Mom is waiting for me at the entrance to the school and we go home. Before, Mom let me stay a little while in the street. Now when I say Mom let me go out and play, Mom doesn't answer me, but when we go by the store she buys me the fire truck we saw last week. And I don't know where she gets the money because Granddad says that there's not a cent in this house and that he has to come up with all the money we spend, because he says that my dad is inconsiderate and irresponsible for having left without thinking about his son and his wife, no matter how many ideals he might have. I don't know what these ideals are that my dad has, and I ask my mom if my dad is sick or something. But she barely hears me, since she gets under the bedspread to hear the radio that sounds terrible with so many whistles and snorts that it seems like it's going to explode. And we go home with the fire truck, and now I don't care so much that Mom won't let me go down to the street although I wish that my friends could see how the siren goes off when it runs along the floor and how a lamp on top of the cab shoots off lights as if it really were a fire truck. And when we were returning with my fire truck is when we saw the man. The man was a very old, old man, and when we saw him he was sitting on one of the park benches, and he was looking very intently at a little leaf that had fallen on his leg from the tree. I don't know why I thought that if he liked the leaf from the tree so much that he was also going to like the little green cricket that I was carrying in a matchbox but I went over and I showed him my little cricket. And it didn't scare him, instead he picked it up and told me that crickets don't live in the grass like people say but rather in matchboxes with holes in them so that they can breathe and it is in the matchboxes where they feel happiest because they know that outside the matchbox there is a little boy who ever so often is going to give them food and pet them on their stomachs and that is how they feel happy. And the old man got quiet and then he told me that although you never know why, sometimes crickets are very foolish and they might miss the place where they were born, the grass moving in the wind, singing in the cool of the evening, and then they try to escape or they die of sadness. Although he wouldn't know what to do, says the old man, if he were a cricket. He said all that and my mother gave him the last coin that was left in her change purse. When we got home my aunt wasn't there. And it was very late when my aunt returned. Grandmother got up from the table and without saying a word started to cry. Then Granddad also stopped eating and took his belt off and said that they don't have respect for anything, and he went toward my aunt's room. I have never seen how they beat an adult, and even though my aunt is very young she already is a big person who works in an office and goes out alone and all those things. But that's how it was that Granddad got up from the table and took off his belt. I had never seen my granddad as serious as he was that night either, and while I was sitting there eating I heard my aunt's shouts and the shouts of my granddad who was saying a very funny thing, malted cocktail, or malted cockatiel. And I imagined one of those little colorful birds swimming around in a big malted milkshake. And I don't know why Granddad won't let my aunt go out again with the malted cockatiel, maybe there's a person with that name whom Granddad doesn't like, because he shouts a lot. And Grandmother orders him to be quiet and tells him to be careful, and he begins to close the windows and I still hear Grandmother's sobs and also the noise that the belt makes when it hits and I felt like getting up from the table and grabbing Granddad by the arm and telling him don't hit my aunt anymore. What's happening, Mom. Nothing, dear, keep eating, keep eating. Nothing is wrong, your granddad is angry with your aunt. Eat, your food is getting cold. But I didn't feel like eating and I just sat there, stiff, waiting. And Mom didn't move or eat either. Until a long time later when Granddad came out and looked at us, ran his hand across his brow and put on his belt and sat down at the table again, and there he was stirring the rice with his fork making mountains, valleys, roads in the beans, but he didn't eat either. And I saw that his eyes were red and I felt sorry for Granddad, but I also felt sorry for my aunt. And when I had gone to bed I started thinking that when I was a big person like my aunt and I was working in an office and a granddad beat me with a belt, I would put all my things in a suitcase and I would leave home to wander around, to see the world, to look for my dad. And I don't know why, but I began to cry and I was crying for a long time until I finally fell asleep. And this morning I was sure that I wasn't going to see my aunt again, that she would leave forever. That's why I went to look for her in her room to say goodbye and to tell her that if she wanted that I would defend her. And I was waiting for her for a long time until she came out acting very nervous and when I went to speak to her it seemed that nothing had happened the day before. She laughed a lot, she ran her hand through my hair and said that the man had gone away, that the man had gone away, she shouted. And I thought that she was talking about the cricket man, but it seems that it was someone else, someone whom my aunt didn't love and whom she was glad had left. And I thought that adults are impossible to understand and I asked her if it hurt a lot. What. Granddad's belt, I tell her. Then she laughs out loud and tells me that a little, not much. But you were screaming a lot. But I wasn't screaming because it hurt but because we were arguing. Arguing about what. But at that moment a man wearing glasses arrived and grabbed my aunt by the shoulders. And Mother let out a scream from the kitchen and came to hug him. And I don't know who this unshaven man is who is lifting me in the air. He's your father, says my aunt. He's your father, she repeats. And when he puts me down on the ground again I run to the balcony and I look down at the street where everyone seems to be celebrating. They hug each other and they run around. A few boys pick up some iron rails and start hitting the parking meters. I can see all this from the balcony. And when the parking meters break, the coins roll down the street. And then I see that the old cricket man is picking up the coins that fell out on the sidewalk. And I run down the stairs and I start helping the old man put the coins in his pocket and I tell him that it seems like Havana isn't as big as they say because my dad had managed to come back.

Translated by Victoria L. McCard

OTHER TALES FROM CONTEMPORARY CUBA

GO FIGURE

For Nancy

I could watch everything Miss Betty did. Not out of any particular curiosity. Hardly. It was out of boredom, a boredom as huge as the Capitol Building. I've had my foot in a cast for almost two months, and I've still got a ways to go with it. So I don't leave my bay window, I might as well be chained to it, just like in the movie with James Stewart, that actor who always has to play the good guy. My grandmother used to say your face is a portrait of your soul. True enough, Miss Betty's face is like the face of a sparrow with a cat watching it, I'd say. Well, in the movie it's more or less the same thing. This James Stewart, with his kindly face, has his leg in a cast and amuses himself looking out the window. All of a sudden, boom, he realizes that something very strange is happening in the building across the way, one of those buildings with a lot of little windows and a fire escape. Where Miss Betty lives there's no fire escape because in the first place it's not in the Bronx or anywhere like that, it's in a tenement in Old Havana, you know. And in the second place because it's on the ground floor. But it's the same thing. What James Stewart discovers without moving from his armchair is nothing less than a murder and since the plot has to thicken, it doesn't occur to him to call the police or anything, or else he does call and they tell him to get lost, I don't remember which anymore. The main thing is that he starts doing some freelance detective work and begins to phone the other guy, the assassin, who has the kind of face you'd expect, emanating evil from time to time and all that, and finally the devil really gets into the bad guy and he's ready to tear James Stewart to bits, and the cops show up right then, which is always really stupid in mystery novels, but they get there just in time and of course, the happily-ever-after ending, everyone is pleased as punch except you know who, and then James Stewart with his good guy's face probably tells a joke, and the curtain falls with a final burst of laughter all around, like in those American movies that waver somewhere between Greek tragedy and the Three Stooges. Come to think of it, I'm not sure whether I should tell this story as a tragedy or a comedy. Miss Betty is about fifty thousand years old and leads a completely solitary life. Every evening, after she gets home from work, she makes herself a cup of tea without sugar, waters the plants, and then stands there with the watering can, looking out into space, for over half an hour. I swear it. Then she pulls a rocking chair up close to the door that opens onto the patio to take in the fresh air, the night dew. My grandmother said that it isn't good for you to breathe dew, but nobody'd better go and say that to Miss Betty. And anyway, I don't think she has anything else to do. She just stays there, rocking, until people start going out to work the night shift. Then she pulls in the rocking chair and turns out all the lights except the one in the entry hall. Day after day, the same operation. The truth is that she must feel lonely as hell. As far as I know, she's had three husbands. The first died of an embolism in a whorehouse, she herself tells the story, but Miss Betty would never dream of saying whore, so she says "women in the life," a phrase I've never understood very well, because isn't everyone in the life? I'll leave that problem alone. She lost the first husband that way, and the second one was run over by a train. Gentlemen, that's what you call bad luck. How may people do you know who've been run over by a train! I've only heard of Anna Karenina. And that was because she threw herself onto the tracks. But in Miss Betty's case, pow, a train comes and cuts her second husband in half, and he seems to have been a great guy, the one meant for her, and he was giving her industrial quantities of happiness, but that happened during capitalism and almost nobody in the neighborhood remembers it now. Although I imagine Miss Betty does, especially when she's out there in the dew. Right? The third one, the last chance, the lucky number, the triad, the three-cornered hat, the three musketeers, the three little pigs, the three Villalobos, the three Marias, good things come in threes, the Matamoros Trio, the three of hearts, the great one-two-three dance step that guy Hegel invented, the third time's the charm, brought the final catastrophe. The third little pig left on the Mariel boat lift, and that time the one who almost had a heart attack was Miss Betty. Because she's very revolutionary and does all the committee work. Imagine, she even picks up bottles to recycle for raw material and everything. Nobody ever expected Mario Rodríguez to leave her stranded, to her own devices, as they say. The guy never got involved in anything, but he didn't fool anyone. An opportunist, I tell you. When he did a plumbing job, a private one, I mean, he'd stick it to his client, deep into center field, he nailed you, fifteen shots of rum just to change a washer, that really shows you what he was like. But Miss Betty, going from home to work, from work to home, she probably didn't know the half of it. And on top of it all she loved the guy. Those things happen. So, she almost died of sadness. For three days she didn't leave the house, but one thing's for sure, Miss Betty doesn't want to hear of marrying again. Things that hurt, you have to pull out by the roots, even though a part of you goes with them. The bad part of it is that she's as lonely as a street dog, just like the words to that tango. That's why she's having all these problems. Miss Betty, well, of course she's no Miss, I mean her virginity, which she must have lost back in the Machado's time, because otherwise she's very well-mannered and discreet.[4] That's something my grandmother used to say: a discreet person doesn't butt in where they aren't wanted, just the opposite of what I'm doing now. They call her "Miss" because she's been a schoolteacher all her life, and the neighborhood kids always knew her by that name and it stuck. She isn't "Betty" out of any imperialistic verbal takeover, out of cultural penetration, or anything like that; what happened is that when she was born, in the time when jazz was young, they named her Bertilda, and that's too hard a name for kids, everyone must realize that, because, well, Miss Betty was really patriotic and respected traditions even before, when the bad guys were in power. That's why she almost died of embarrassment when Mario

---

[4] Gerardo Machado y Morales was the President of Cuba, 1925-1933.

Rodríguez, the third little pig I told you about who was moreover her umpteenth husband, sold his toolbox and went to Yuma. Now, you know Yuma is street slang for the pesky North. I have no idea where that name came from, but it's pretty good, because first you let out the YU so it seems you're going to say it nicely and then you suddenly finish it off in that tasteless, hick way they have of speaking up there. So it's more graphic to say Mario Rodríguez left for Yuma, bringing the final A out of your wide-open mouth as you let all the air out of your lungs with a great big dose of scorn. As though you thought you were talking about a mouse. Although I guarantee you that some mice are better than people. But I'm getting off the point. Miss Betty doesn't talk about Mario Rodríguez that way, or about anyone, to her it was as if he had died. She never mentioned the guy again, or let even one silly little tear fall. Good for her, right? What I don't understand is why she's so bent on living alone, since she's still got plenty of fire in her. It's a real drag to live alone like that. And it's why all those things happen to her. The little kids climb up on her wooden fence and pull the planks loose, and it just stays like that. Her water tanks leak, and you can't expect her to crawl around and change the valves on them, so they keep leaking. The breeze knocks her TV antenna out of place, and now she can't get channel 2 anymore. Until some neighbor's heart breaks in three pieces and he climbs up on the roof to fix it for her. You see, Miss Betty doesn't like to go around bothering people or asking for things. A tragedy, one hell of a hullabaloo. From my observation point I attended the opening: a cry as if she'd seen Boris Karloff in person, crockery flying through the air, broken glass, and a big hustle-bustle in Miss Betty's kitchen.

"What happened?" I asked her, and in passing I showed her my foot in its cast so she'd understand right away that I couldn't really help; she was defenseless in her enemy's claws.

"A mouse, a little mouse in the cupboard," she answered, and added for the sake of clarity, *"in my kitchen."*

This last thing she said like a trumpet announcing the last judgment. I opened my eyes wide and bit my lower lip in a simultaneous sign of surprise, nausea, and solidarity, a grimace that no words could have replaced. We Cubans are like that, half the time we'd rather gesticulate than converse. We must have gotten that from the Italians, through Columbus. All you have to do is see one of those Italian movies to tell whether we seem alike or not, especially the Sicilians. Listen to an argument in the house of a Cuban family and you won't deny we're just alike. I'm not kidding. This is an original theory of mine, but nobody has paid any attention to it yet. If you do, you're the first. Just imagine that scene, with Miss Betty holding on to her housedress as though it was going to split open from top to bottom, one foot bare and the other in a slipper. A hideous countenance. Complete desperation, you know how that is. With her hair so disheveled you could hardly imagine it, her eyes whirling out of their orbits, and her throat about to let loose another jungle yell, she could very well have been some sort of Anna Magnani, seconds before shouting *mamma mia!,* but Miss Betty couldn't say such a thing for two reasons, obvious ones, believe me.[5] First and foremost, because she's got a very clear sense of the absurd, and second, because as far as I know, she doesn't speak Italian, even though she's read Dante's *Inferno* about eighteen times. So what she said was "Oh my God!" five or six times in a row before closing the kitchen door. Speaking of hell: that isn't the end of it. Two minutes later she came back out into the hall armed to the teeth with a pile of newspapers and a broom. The newspapers really intrigued me, I won't pretend they didn't.

"The hunt has begun," she said sotto voce, and I raised my arms in a gesture that meant this: Courage, courage!

Miss Betty began to cover everything with the newspapers. Would the house catch on fire? The worst of that is that I would be the first victim. You know, because my foot's in a cast. Gentlemen, suddenly a light went on in my head. Miss Betty was covering all the conduits

---

[5] Anna Magnani was an Italian star of stage and screen.

through which the undesirable entity might reestablish himself in her kitchen. With tremendous patience, she took piles of paper and covered the drainpipes, the flues, the holes in the window, the nooks and crannies of the flowerboxes, the garbage can, the narrow space between the tanks of butane.

"It's got to get out of here this very day," said Miss Betty out loud, and I felt obligated to respond, considering that I was her only available audience for a million miles around.

"It's probably more than one. They have their young all over the place," I said, and realized immediately I'd stuck my foot in it. Miss Betty looked at me as though all the mice in the neighborhood were lodged in my person. Or at least as though I were their key accomplice. I displayed an idiotic smile to smooth over my blunder, but she wasn't looking at me anymore. She kept on bustling around with her newspapers. Well, what happened was I started to understand her strategy. It was to force the mouse to leave the cupboard, turn the corner very nicely into the hall I told you about, take the direction of the patio, and of it's own accord get lost in a gutter *per secula seculorum*.[6] She didn't want to have to draw blood like some Lady Macbeth. Well, what do you think of that! Bye, little mouse, there's no need for rancor, we can still be good friends. I almost died laughing at that. So I didn't miss a single move as she emptied the cupboard, pot by pot, can by can, bottle by bottle, rag by rag, and damn, there went that obstinate little mouse at the speed of sound, from comer to corner, crawling over here, climbing over there, confused in the face of the mountains of newsprint. "How the lay of the land has changed!" it probably said to itself, running at the highest velocity, like a rocket, and Miss Betty jumping up and down with the broom in her hand, she looked like an Apache, I swear it on my mother's grave.

"Out, out, damn mouse!"

It was one hell of a chaotic scene.

The mouse, just like that, when it got tired of the little game,

[6] For ever and ever

went straight to its private rooms in the cupboard. Well, this running back and forth I'm telling you about was just the beginning. The next Sunday, she started the whole process over again, with the newsprint bills, the cardboard dikes, and the broom over her shoulder.

"You don't think the mouse has won?" I asked.

Miss Betty looked at me seriously, though she didn't seem mad or anything. I don't know how to explain it. It was as though she were under a spell, as my grandmother would have said. At it again, she emptied the cupboard, but in a more careful, better-planned way. The way she set things out this time, in the shape of the Great Wall of China, gave the intruder only one possibility: peaceful surrender. No violence. Who would have calculated that, splash! It would fall in the flowerpot with no dirt in it, full of water, a medieval moat, considering the tiny size of that mouse. Miss Betty marched along, holding the broom up like a lance, all ready to deliver the final blow. Then she saw the mouse's soaked and totally defenseless body. We can assume its frightened eyes were fixed on its executioner. Imagine the result: Miss Betty held out the broom, which from being a homicidal weapon turned into a life-saving ramp, and the shipwreck victim ran up it to take refuge once again in the cupboard, *her kitchen* cupboard.

"It would have been a crime to liquidate him like that," she said, and watched me with a mixture of shame and defiance.

"Of course," I answered with my usual stupid little smile. Numerical superiority. Sportsmanship. "Why don't you try a cat?"

Now Miss Betty's gaze made me feel like a professional torturer.

"And how do I get rid of the cat afterward?" she murmured.

Operation Mousetrap began the next day. The first bait was a little piece of lunchmeat that disappeared without producing a victim. Next she tried cheese, like in the cartoons. And the same thing happened. Finally, she used a really appetizing piece of bread dipped in milk. Each time the trap was sprung and the mouse was just fine, thank you.

"A diet to gain weight," I said, and nobody laughed. "This mouse is a marvelous animal. He's outsmarting you."

"Put yourself in his place," she answered in an indecipherable tone.

"What?"

"Just that: a delicious lunch and then what awaits you? Death!"

"Chilling! When you put it that way, it seems really horrible."

"It is."

"And why don't you pardon him? He's earned it."

This time she answered angrily: "You're crazy. Typhus, bubonic plague. He's got to go somehow, it doesn't matter how."

But as time passed, I think she got used to the idea of sharing her kitchen with that mouse. She stopped chatting with me and started talking to herself: "Poison in the corners. No way. That's a disgusting system. Then he dies just anywhere and you don't even realize it. Only the stench clues you in. How disgusting!" Every day Miss Betty got more pensive, more melancholy. Thinner than a new shoot of sugar cane. That early morning when the sound of the mousetrap and the screeching of the mouse awakened half of humanity in Miss Betty's house, that is to say, the noise awakened Miss Betty, I was still in my watchtower, with a face like James Stewart and everything. The hunt seemed to have come to an end.

"I'd rather not face *that*," she exclaimed without addressing anyone in particular, but I've already told you, it was about three in the morning and I felt as though she and I, if you don't count the mouse, were the only people awake on the planet Earth. I saw that she was opening the cupboard door slowly, and now her shout was a combination of horror and relief, "The tail!"

"What?" I shouted for my part.

"He lost his tail and managed to escape."

Miss Betty leaned out into the hall and then she did address me, with a lugubrious voice, like in a funeral parlor:

"His luck has begun to run out."

I started to think the strangest thing, something like the things that hurt when you have to pull them out by the roots, and suddenly she said:

"By the roots."

Thought transference—you think?

It wasn't until much later that events came to a head and I found out what happened in the end. Miss Betty had gone to look for her can of tea in the cupboard. Absentmindedly she pulled open the door and without meaning to, she caught the mouse—whose name we never knew—in the hinges. I want to tell you that he died instantaneously and with dignity. He left no heirs. I didn't see Miss Betty for about a million days. When she finally came out to water the plants, she stumbled all of a sudden on my gaze.

"He escaped from everything to end up dying by a fluke. Go figure," she said.

Miss Betty started sobbing, and she wept, wept, wept, as never before, I had never, nobody had ever seen her cry.

Translated by Leslie Bary

THE BEATLES VS. DURAN DURAN

I've always been green with envy of the people who dream well. But I was a hopeless case. I've consulted with a psychiatrist in order to discover the cause of my nighttime banality. In the hospital I gave my neurons a workout with a few sessions of tell me about yourself, hypnotism, and even acupuncture, although I didn't get many results for my efforts. After the sessions, all I had to show was a prescription for forty trifluoperazines[7] and luckily, a diagnosis that my problem wasn't a lack of imagination, but rather, something deeper. In my neighborhood, this type of analysis is known as the discovery of the obvious. My shrink was satisfied, but I would have felt better if the doctor had guaranteed that I would have nighttime visions, extravagant nightmares or even the same dragons as my colleagues. Nothing gives me a worse inferiority complex than that unfortunate moment every morning when some dimwit who, you know—the type who can't do anything right during the day—comes in and announces that "Last night I had an incredible dream." And he proceeds with no further introduction to tell everybody a Buñuelesque, absurd and morbid tale full of watches melted like butter or chickens with drawers in their bellies á la Dalí. You ask yourself, how is that possible?

For years and years I've put up with it. Envy is gnawing away at my soul. Invariably the dreams of those people are in Technicolor and Cinemascope. And I, the best I can do, in black and white, eight millimeter, dreaming every night about the same things that happen to me during the day. In Cuba there are ten million people, and without going into the statistics, I feel safe in saying that I am the only person on the whole island who uses file material, reruns, literal transmissions of

---

[7] Trifluoperazine is a phenothiazine tranquilizer used especially in the treatment of psychotic conditions like schizophrenia.

daily life, the comings and goings of her department, and the everyday of home sweet home for her dreams. What a bore, what a disgrace. No one can deny it. I'm embarrassed to confess what happens next, but I should admit that for as long as I've lived, I've yet to see a pink dragon.

Wait, the worst is yet to come. Ever since I was a little girl I always get a jump on myself. I'm not talking about premonitions, oracles of Delphi or anything like that, but rather something much more prosaic. If at school they announced a math quiz, the night before I would dream that I was seated at my desk with a terrifyingly blank sheet of paper in front of me, to add, subtract, and answer from memory the damn seven tables. When the hour of the real quiz finally arrived, I couldn't avoid the exhausting impression that I'd already been through all that.

For example, one Monday last month I found out that someone was going to observe my class the following Thursday. They blew the whistle on me at a very inopportune time. The Thursday in question dealt with some putrid subject matter, if you'll let me talk like that in public about synecdoches and metonyms. What else can I say? I spent three nights, one after the other, rehashing the same point in the program, with the added agony of counting out the time for the entire lecture so that it would end up coinciding with the recess bell and, what's worse, Assistant Dean Justina crashed my nightmare three nights in a row. A medieval torture. The Inquisition was a cakewalk compared to this. In summary, when faced with any fucked-up problem (pardon the expression), my subconscious throws my early mornings into a trance looking for a solution. Lord only knows how many times I divorced Evelio while asleep like a log before I signed the legal papers in the notary's office on San Rafael Street. Freud would have been dumbfounded by my clinical chart. And of course the situation is complicated by the appearance of the signs.

This thing about the signs isn't an exclusive of mine. I share the copyright with my family. In my house, we're very easy-going and when we get an idea into our heads or we have some task pending, someone always gets the bright idea of writing it in caveman letters on the wall, on whatever wall is closest to hand. We never bother to erase it and if memory serves, in thirty years this house hasn't known a paint brush, so the signs have been accumulating, one on top of the other, causing great confusion, some even appear with *fe de erratas,* you die laughing and some things make you want to cry: **Monday the 15th Grandfather's funeral,** and immediately after **don't eat my pudding.** Above the TV it's noted **remember kid to brush your teeth before going to the dentist** and opposite that **volunteer work on Sunday;** along the hall you can still read this **change your life said Rimbaud** and on the window in my room, in my own handwriting it says **arrives tomorrow** and the name is scratched out so that now I am unable to remember who was arriving on that lost morning of the past; in the bathroom you can still make out verb conjugations in Latin and above them **next week buy anniversary present;** every time a new visitor arrives he's taken aback by the front door where esoteric capital letters spell out: **restore** *The Garden of Earthly Delights.*

To make a long story short, because of that bad habit of the family billboards all of a sudden my dreams come with signs. All I have to do is close my eyes and the **Dream of the Annual Self-Evaluation** is announced, and I myself appear in my nightmare editing the report that I'm supposed to rewrite the following day. Working double time, ladies and gentlemen. Or what's worse: the **Dream of the Department Meeting** that I then have to sit through again, exactly the same, with details, everyone saying the same things. When I say the same things it's not an exaggeration. What I wouldn't give to dream that I'm walking along the Rampa[8] wrapped in a gauze tunic or that I liquidate some of my colleagues in the above-mentioned department with poison mushrooms, or at the very least that I find myself one day with my classroom full of little green dwarves. But no. Always the same old same old. I'd like to clarify that this redundancy does not escape me,

---

[8] The Rampa is the section of 23rd St. running from L St. (in the center of Vedado) down to the Malecón (ocean front). This is one of the busiest blocks in Havana.

it's intentional. I'd love to see you in my place, not changing channels, day in and day out with the same schedule of programs. In short, since I have the opportunity to see the previews in my dreams, in the mornings I already know what awaits me.

Like the other night for example. I arrived rather late from the university, I fixed myself something to eat, and I went to bed armed with a cheese sandwich, a pen and five tons of exams to grade. The moment I put my head on the pillow I noticed a new sign written in red marker on my enamel bookcase: **Mommy, don't forget to sign the form for me.** The form itself was stuck with a piece of scotch-tape to my *Larousse Illustrated Dictionary*. Without getting up, I was able to make out that it had something to do with registering for General Military Service.

In summary, what happened was that all night long I couldn't get my mind off the damn problem of that form and I was dreaming about a frightening argument with my daughter, Pilar.

A nightmare of the worst kind. I suppose that it won't come as a surprise to the audience that the world premier of this nightmare was accompanied by the habitual sign that introduces my dreams. Let me add however that this sign was blood curdling. Its design was Gothic but its language belonged to the dialect of the Havana native: **Evil Spell between Mother and Her Only Little Girl.** Promising, right?

The point of departure of the argument was the blessed form that I REFUSE TO SIGN, according to Pilar, who mocked me with a contorted mouth and hair that looked like something out of a Tarzan movie. I didn't keep my mouth shut either. I've always been famous for having a sharp tongue, and my daughter is a chip off the old block. We went at it, one might say, tooth and nail.

According to her exact words, I have turned into a well-to-do reactionary old lady who never gets up off her ass and whose only worry is that the goblets not get broken in the sideboard. Then it was my turn in the dream. I ignored the comment about the wine glasses because so few are left that they're hardly worth the trouble. That I refuse to sign the form and the reactionary old lady part both seem exaggerated, due to the heat of the moment, and I made that known to Pilar. In passing, I informed her that she was a snotty-nosed know-it-all who wanted to make all her own decisions and that I wasn't going to stand for it. Last but not least, relating to the comment regarding her mother's anatomy, I hit her with a recurring phrase from the repertoire of the Cuban mother.[9] A sentence that in addition to being untrue, was abusive on my part. But you are already well aware of what household fireworks are like.

It took Pilar a moment to recover from my attack. Thinking that I had breached the enemy's weak flank, I then made the mistake of using a protective tone. I had the bad idea (and I'm still in the arms of Morpheus, mind you) of raising the stock argument that dominates every generational confrontation: "When I was your age..."

After the third word my advantage was lost. Pilar pounced like a tiger and gave me a lashing with the family resumé. She went through the whole family tree from the last century until the day before yesterday. First she went back to the example of Great Aunt Beatrice who had creatively withstood twenty-two years of captivity among the Guaicurúe Indians of the Argentine pampas as the battle-hardened concubine of the chief who had taught her such unorthodox customs as how to throw the *bolas* (she had a Dead-eye Dick aim); then Pilar invoked Grandmother Leonor and recounted how in her adolescence she rejected the marriage proposal of a German baron in order to defend her freedom and set sail to seek her fortune in America, hidden as a stowaway in the hold of a French ship, in the middle of World War I; she went down the list, of course, to the wife of Uncle Federico, that passionate Teté, a tobacconist who went on strike in the 30s and who single-handedly supported a family of twelve sons when Uncle Federico was arrested for being a communist in 1952; and with that, leaving ancient history behind, what about cousin Margarita behind the wheel of a fire-engine red convertible back when it wouldn't have occurred

---

[9] The recurring phrase is "No sabes todavía lavarte el culo" ("You don't even know how to wipe your ass yet").

to anyone to defy social conventions, a major scandal. Until arriving finally at the *coup de grace,* and you, my very own mother, ignoring advice and restrictions had gone to pick coffee up in the mountains when you were still a mere child.

I could barely respond. I heard my own voice, which retained a tinge of irony, retorting that the retelling of our family's background in women's liberation was fine, but it still seemed excessive to me that the apple of my eye wanted to renounce her pursuit of a nice career in Art History in order to fire rounds from a four-barrel machine gun.

That morning I woke up in a foul mood. How could my subconscious do this to me, and turn me into this conventional **mommy** who wants her only "little girl" out of danger and tied to her apron strings? I couldn't forgive myself for saying that stinging sentence, you know the one I'm talking about, THAT ONE about "such a nice career." I made myself sick.

However, I also couldn't forget the insults that Pilar had hurled at me in the dream.

That was the reason for the hangdog face that I was showing the world the next morning, as if I really had fought, while I was eating breakfast and Pilar came in with her tape player going full blast with the treble up as high as it would go. A screeching was coming from it that would have pierced the eardrums of the Sphinx of Giza.

Pilar sat down at the table and it wasn't enough that she ate the piece of toast that I had already spread with jam for myself, she also put her tape player on top of my lesson plans, grade book and other paperwork.

"What's wrong with you this morning?" she asked.

"Ummmmmm," I barely answered, taking advantage of the fact that my mouth was full.

"O.K., O.K., you're right," she answered without thinking too much about logic. Then she threatened me:

"I want you to listen to this song from the beginning. Let's see what you think of it."

I saw with horror that she was pressing the rewind button, that the cassette was moving backwards, her index finger pushed the play button and that peculiar mix of shrieks, whip cracking and BOOM BOOM BOOM started all over again.

I raised my eyebrows as high as I could and said:

"When I was young," the sentence sounded abominable to me from the beginning, "the music sounded a whole lot better."

Pilar looked me over from head to foot as if a dinosaur had suddenly decided to make a commentary on contemporary art. I got the impression that Pilar didn't think it necessary to use convincing arguments, so she merely made use of a mocking little voice and she tapped out:

"So let me see, the Beatles were brilliant, of course, blah, blah, blah, and this that and the other, and everything after them…"

"Pilar, honey, I hope you're not going to try to convince me that these guys are the musicians of the century. And to think that in my generation it cost us blood, sweat, and tears to hear a Beatles' song. And you have the luxury of…"

"What are you talking about, Mom?"

"Nothing. It's just that everything is **too easy** for you guys."

I couldn't avoid the emphasis I put on those words. I tried to fix it, but it was too late. Pilar puffed up like an angry cat.

"I already know that song, letter and verse. Oh, Mom, the world is changing."

"Yes, yes," I answered, returning her volley. "I know it by heart too. But, Pilar, fashion always repeats itself to the point of…"

It's not for naught that Pilar is my daughter, so she slammed my shot back at me and scored a point:

"You yourself have taught me that it returns, Mom, and I quote, 'although on a higher rung of the spiral,' end of quote, Engels, 'The Dialectic,' *Chosen Works, Volume III*. Look at yourself in the mirror. You've been left behind. You're getting old."

"End of quote, Pilar the Wise, *Complete Works, Volume XVII.*"

"Don't try to be funny, Mom. And face facts. I'm telling you this in all seriousness."

Can you believe it! I was clearly in retreat.

"Listen to me, what's in style now is hard rock, wavy hair, and loose clothes. You dress just like all those old relics you work with."

That was an evil statement. Nonetheless, my daughter had scored another point. I felt like a mummy, a decrepit old hag, the spitting image of Methuselah. The score was two to nothing. I openly recognized my disadvantage and looked at myself suspiciously in the mirror. What I saw reflected there was the image of a middle-aged woman, with a skirt that was tight around the hips, big square-heeled shoes, and a flowery blouse that was also too tight. I have to confess that I detested what I saw, but I still tried to defend myself:

"You wouldn't want me to turn into a disgraceful old lady."

"A what kind of old lady? I don't understand you."

Suddenly I felt there was an abyss between Pilar and me that I didn't feel capable of bridging. At some other more opportune moment I would try to close that gap that sometimes opens up between people who love each other, at times because of communication problems and at times for other more serious causes.

"Some day I'll explain it to you. It's a saying from my generation. And so you'll feel complete: I have the sensation that the Angel of Death just came in, so I'm getting out of here."

While I gathered up my paper work, Pilar was looking at me with an expression of genuine surprise. She must have recovered quickly though because before I could get to the corner, I heard my daughter yelling at me from the balcony (it couldn't wait until later), wielding her cassette player.

"I like the Beatles too! But these guys are popular NOW!"

My curiosity was aroused. I suppose that exchange of words must have seemed a little strange to the President of Committee[10] who was witnessing the whole scene from her front doorway, but I couldn't overlook that musical gap. So I shouted back at her:

---

[10] CDR is the Committee for the Defense of the Revolution, the officially sanctioned neighborhood watchdog group that is on the lookout for any behavior that might be considered "counterrevolutionary."

"What's their name?"

"Duran Duran," Pilar finally responded with a scream.

The second part of this story has a completely different setting. The afternoon following the gladiatorial bout with Pilar, they sent me on an unexpected trip to Nicaragua. I was so thrilled that I simply forgot the dream about the form, the damn form itself, which was still visible on the spine of my *Larousse Illustrated Dictionary,* and also the fight to the death between the Beatles and Duran Duran, with a slight lead going to the latter, even though the Beatles held the home field advantage.

I feel obligated to recognize (hara-kiri while you wait) that I didn't think about the whole question again until I was just about to return to Havana and my friend, Miguel, invited me to pick coffee on a farm north of Managua.

"Pick coffee" is the expression that we Cubans use, but the Nicaraguans don't say it like that. They talk about "cutting the little red bean." Whether you cut the bean or pick it, it's the same thing. No matter how you say it, what does matter is that they put me in the time machine and I was deposited in a remote corner of my memory, going back twenty years, in that far away time when I was with my high school friends picking coffee in the hills of Upper Mayarí.[11] Twenty years is nothing, the Tango master Gardel's sophism still goes directly to the grain. Given the opportunity to spend three days in the mountains "cutting the little red bean," I completely forgot about my incipient arthritis, my migraines, my office ulcer, and all the other aches and pains that I suffered from. I did, however, remember Pilar and her criticisms.

I don't want you to think that the change of setting freed this second part from its signs, the news of light sleep and fits of the subconscious. The night before leaving for the coffee farm, I dreamed that I was in the mountains, hanging from a coffee bush over a cliff, with my bag half empty and trying, in vain, to reach a red bean that was eluding me at the top of a bush that had already been picked clean.

---

[11] In Holguín Province.

Beside me was working another girl from the brigade who was a super picker; I watched her with that feeling that usually gets mixed up in a no man's land between envy and the desire to imitate. I couldn't see her face, but when she finally spoke, I discovered that she was my daughter, Pilar, wearing black leather boots that were shining like asphalt (anyone who has spent half a minute on a muddy hill will be able to calculate the feasibility of this description), an *Industriales*[12] team cap that had seen better days, and her bag overflowing with ripe beans, all with the same red color. Everything seemed to indicate that the discussion that had taken place on our home field was not finished, even when its protagonists were now situated in a different theater of operations. Without introductions, prefaces or any advance notice, my daughter began to rant and rave about the topic of the form, I can't believe it, Mom, you, who ran away from Grandmother to pick coffee in the mountains of Oriente, turning a deaf ear to family opinion, a girl merely severing the ties of an improper upbringing, **we're not the same as we were then,** the you that you are now, rotting in with your papers, you don't want to sign the FORM, using the arguments of a Bourgeois old lady with something to lose, picking coffee in the middle of Hurricane Flora isn't the same as taking an artillery course, Mom, please, you're trying to make me believe that they are two very different things, but in the end, you know that they are the same thing. THE SAME THING.

I woke up with a taste between bitter and sweet (like day-old coffee), not in my mouth, but in that metaphorical region that we usually refer to as the heart. I checked my watch and observed the movement of the hands for about two hours. Finally, around three a.m. Miguel came to pick me up, carrying a huge backpack. The trip to the coffee region, crowded together on top of a truck and getting tossed around like sacks of potatoes, lasted more than nine hours. During that journey I was able to test the will of my well-worn bones, which were veterans of cane cutting, militia mobilizations, red Sundays, hurricane

---

[12] "Industriales" is the name of Havana's most important professional baseball team.

warnings and other occupations of that nature.

The transport with its load of talking potatoes reached its destination around noon. Before getting off the truck, the brigade leader asked for a moment of silence to honor the martyrs of the war against Somoza and then we sang the Sandinista anthem.[13] If it had been possible for me to consult with a Chinese wise man, it's probable that he would have interpreted the pandemonium of my feelings, as the result of the age-old trick of the repeating mirrors or the distraction of the butterflies that confuse their dreams with those of Chuang-Tzu[14]; the uncertainty of the new in the middle of a very-well known, familiar context; the turn of the spiral is what my daughter Pilar would call it.

The brigade leader gave the order and we immediately fell into two columns. We entered the rows of coffee bushes in military formation, each one with a basket slung across her shoulder. The time machine began another somersault. I wished that Fifa, or Ada Gloria or any of the girls of that old brigade could have been in it with me. Times change, I muttered under my breath, while the memory of last night's sign burst in: **Dream of the confrontation between two generations.** To tell the truth, a rhetorical title and not at all subtle.

A bush full of little red beans was waiting for me. I hadn't touched a coffee bean in twenty years, but my fingers instantly recovered the reflex, the former motion, and the machinery started to hum as if it had just been greased. If only Pilar could see me now! She'd stop calling her mother an old bag. However, the girl in the row next to mine was not my daughter, but another girl, as young as Pilar, wearing a military uniform, with a basket overflowing with red coffee and a machine gun slung across her back. Beyond her I saw two more, and, at the other end, a group of five or six, all with the uniform, the basket of coffee and the firearm hanging from their shoulders. Miguel noticed my curiosity

---

[13] The Contra War refers to the counterinsurgency in the 1980s in Nicaragua, partially financed by the United States government under the Reagan administration, which fought against the leftist Sandinista government.
[14] 4th century BC Chinese Daoist philosopher.

and explained that there were bands of Contras very nearby. Those girls, who were almost babies, belonged to the Erlinda López Women's brigade and "they cut the little red bean" with their rifles cocked and ready to fire.

The workday ended at sunset and we gathered in a ranch house to measure how much coffee we had picked. It turns out that age and experience do count for something after all. It's fair to say, going straight to the point, that I picked a quantity of coffee worthy of a Nobel Prize. In the meantime, one of those Women's Brigade girls had sat down next to me with her AKA on her lap and her ammo belts crossing her chest in the classic Pancho Villa style. She seemed surprised that I had picked so much; my shoes and polished fingernails betrayed my urban, bureaucratic origin.

"You've cut coffee before," the girl wasn't quite asking, because her intonation contained a clearly affirming inflection.

"Yes," I allowed, swelling with pride, all modesty aside. "But more than twenty years ago."

Her eyes opened wide, somewhat incredulously. Then I added: "In Cuba."

The girl looked at me with a huge smile of devotion, and said:

"Next time we'll be in El Salvador."

It was now my turn to have my mouth drop open. Only then did I notice that, in addition to the AKA rifle, she was carrying in her military belts a tiny little tape player. She followed my gaze and interpreted it for herself. With a mud-covered fingernail, she pressed the play button and allowed a strident sound to escape.

"Who is that?" I asked. In my heart of hearts I knew this was a superfluous question, because I had already been overcome by a sneaking suspicion. Let's say I had a strong hunch.

"Duran Duran," the girl answered and added with a friendly familiarity that made me feel twenty years younger, "I'll bet you like them a lot."

Then I responded a little timidly with another question that I was hoping to be able to convert into an affirmation:

"And I'll bet that you like the Beatles."

"You bet I do, girl."

With the same muddy fingernail, she pushed another button and fast-forwarded the tape. This is the end of the second part of the story, with background music from my generation and everything, although I think that the word **generation** should be abolished from my vocabulary. And I guess that you have already figured out that in my next dream the Beatles and Duran Duran are probably going to end up in a tie.

Translated by Victoria L. McCard

KID BURURÚ AND THE CANNIBALS

My fortieth birthday began only a few seconds after midnight, with the peculiar sound of the button on the tape player. Very softly, so the kids wouldn't wake up, "Strawberry Fields Forever" filled the room, the sheets, and all the secret places inside me.

"This is your first present from me," said Marcelo.

Early in the morning another familiar noise woke me. Marcelo was knocking himself out working on the car, trying to get it to start. The open window let me see, from my bed, how his immaculate robe was being smeared with dirty grease from the motor. But that disheartening vision was overshadowed by the sight of my children, standing in the doorway, with an artificial and comic rigidity, singing the traditional birthday song, *"Las mañanitas."*

"Let's get this show on the road!" yelled Marcelo, as he passed through the hall like a hurricane. He stopped for a moment and said, "I'll take the kids, and what are you going to do with your day off?"

I racked my brain thinking.

"Interview a tribe of cannibals, compose an ode, travel to Mars," I answered finally.

Marcelo shook his head from left to right with a look of disbelief and said, "OK, but come back early."

When they had left, I picked up the cigarette butts that had accumulated in the ashtray overnight and threw them in the trash, made the bed, and then I put on a sweater and a pair of jeans that looked like they had been around at least since WWI. I stuck my head out to take a look outdoors. I saw a hazy sun and a few clouds floating by, sweet and lazy, and after thinking on it a bit I decided to take a special trip: from the beginning to the end, from the first stop to the terminal, the complete route of the number 19 bus. All my years as a student, my first love, visits to my grandmother on Reina St., the Cinemateca, my marriage to Enriquito, my career, my job at the hospital, my old life was spent getting on and off the number 19.

It was a good long walk to the first stop. Not that I hadn't done it before. But, ugh, today I was joined by twenty-two little lines around my eyes (*chicken feet* in French), that I didn't have back then, as well as an extra pound or two and a few cavities. Still, what bothered me was being winded. So the first official question that I asked myself, as I waited for the bus to arrive, was: How much do you change as a few years go by? I remember that on the day my cat Robin died, it struck me that my childhood was over. It was already starting to worry me how I would know, before it was too late, when I would begin to grow old.

The bus had also changed. Now it had a blue exterior, recently painted, and shiny bumpers. It looked very sturdy, although I'll admit I preferred the other ones, those strays that seemed like they would fall apart at any moment, with broken windowpanes, leaks, and a frightening noise escaping from their bowels. The old 19s of my adolescence were somehow alive. When the front end would peek around Zapata St., I always imagined the cautious forepaw of some kind of rainproof animal. Maybe, like the others, they had ended up in some secret bone yard after so much careening through the streets of Havana.

I sat down next to the window on the right side, in the last row. I wasn't sure at first, but finally I opted for the right. You'll see why. After leaving the bus stop, the first thing that catches your eye is Sports City and the Shining Fountain. They were on the left, so I had to stretch my neck a little to see the boys, with their practice outfits of shorts and blue tank tops, running along the track, and then the little couple necking at *Paulina's Bidet*. I don't even remember any more who Paulina must have been, but I guess she had a backside sufficiently deserving for the fountain to be given that nickname. It's about eleven a.m. and I had to suppress the desire to light a cigarette that came with the first avalanche of memories. Maybe it was the quiet and the morning freshness that reminded me of the all-nighters studying for my exit exams, with tons of coffee, cigarettes, and crackers with butter. I mentally noted that it had been centuries since I had been up all night with my intellect going full speed. Another bad sign, I told myself.

The travelers on this part of the circuit are usually pretty low-key. I watched their faces and started playing guessing games: athletes, patients coming back from an appointment at the Hospital Surgery Clinic, old women on their routine visits to the cemetery. Full or empty, the number 19 bus goes silently until it comes up to the zoo. The park, fortunately, is on my right, and I can look as much as I like, in spite of the fence and shrubbery. Of course, from the street I can't quite see the lions' cage, but if I get lucky I might make out a sound over the purr of the traffic. Shake a leg, little lion, today's my birthday. The bus slowed down and at last braked for the stop at the park. It was only then that it reached me—the unmistakable sound of an unchecked, dangerous roar. I let myself be just a little afraid, like on that night of initiation that I slept with Pavel and the lions woke us up before dawn.

From that point on, the 19 filled up with children and also with a crowd of kids that were on their way to the university. A group of five or six noticed my worn-out jeans and laughed under their breath. At that age, forty seems a long way off! I think they must have been critiquing the outfit that I had chosen to wear for my escape from the old-age home.

The trek through Nuevo Vedado was only a very short one, while it takes a stretch to get down 26th Ave., as wide as it is and curvy like a roller coaster. One of the kids turned on a boom box: out comes a trumpet riff, (or perhaps it's a sax), after the drawn out "Oh, oh," until Benny's voice breaks in with *"Vida, si pudieras* (pause) *vivir la feliz emoción.*[15]*"* Is he asking me? My heart is obviously still able to beat like a drum. I can hear it, I feel like it's going to split my chest in two, I swallow six times in a row so that I don't make a big scene. Not bad, not bad.

After that the bus took Zapata St. all the way down the side of the

---

[15] "My love, if you could only *(pause)* live the happy feeling."

cemetery. I looked inside and saw myself there, at my grandmother's funeral, or on the afternoons that I went to study with Pavel on the shady benches. Tom, Dick, Harry... I read the headstones quickly and almost without noticing that it was exactly what I used to do years ago.

Close to the corner of 23rd and 12th the little old ladies get off, and a whole bunch of passengers of all kinds get on. It's almost noon, and these are the ones who run home to have lunch and have to get back to work two minutes later. There begins a distinct murmur, one that keeps on growing as the bus goes across El Vedado. This was always the neighborhood that I liked best, especially on Sundays, when it takes on a different flavor than the rest of the week. Before leaving El Vedado, the 19 goes by the hospitals. Little by little, the bus has been filling up with heat and people. The journey was feeling less and less like an outing. I noticed a change in the faces around me. Self-absorbed or with preoccupations that in part I could guess, they showed a certain internal fire that I had forgotten. How is it possible that you forget everything that you learn when you are still young? Imprisoned in the lab, at home. In which cabinet could I have misplaced my sensitivity? I condemn myself to a few psychic lashes for having lost the memory that one time I was there, squeezed in, with three packages under each arm, trying to get to the back door, anxiety-ridden because I would soon be late to the hospital.

Unexpectedly, at the stop of G and Boyeros, two people I knew got on. I hadn't seen them in a thousand years, but they looked just the same: Victor and Enriquito. I just about had a heart attack, and sank back behind my dark mirrored sunglasses. No way in the world did I want them to recognize me. I knew Victor very well because we had been neighbors since we were toddlers. He only has one claim to fame: when we were sophomores, Victor went out to the Rampa with some clippers to cut off the hippies' hair. Need I say more? Victor himself told how he twisted one boy's arm while he gave him a crew cut. "It's that he didn't want me to," he would always explain. That was the first and last fight we had. Afterwards, he abandoned his studies and moved away. I can't help thinking of all of that now, when I see his long blond hair, whipped around a little by the wind.

I know Enriquito even better. We were married for seven years. And here he was, all dressed up in a suit and tie, even though it was twelve noon and the sun was splitting the pavement. Brains and brawn. Enriquito is what you call a real looker. He's always had the body of a fighter, and his face, what can I say? His voice could be heard over the din that filled the bus at that moment. I had loved Enriquito very much, but it had been a doomed marriage from beginning to end. I knew of his running around and ignored it. It was the only way he had to feel confident, act like he was cheating on me with twenty women at a time. What ended up getting to me was that sometimes those girls would comment that he might be big, but it was all show. For some reason that I don't know, he couldn't get it up. I don't even want to think about it. His aggression, the useless parade of doctors, his adventures in deceit. He suffered tremendously, and I was unhappy. Nevertheless, the crisis was sparked by something else. When they selected me to work for two years in Tanzania, Enriquito showed one side in public, the modern and understanding Don Juan, and another side at home: "I don't feel like letting you go, here the one in charge is me, the man." When I came back from the trip, Enriquito had finished the divorce process. In spite of it all, both of us cried and cried.

The bus braked noisily in front of the Veterinary School, and two young women with a poodle stepped on. The first to charge was Enriquito. He quickly thrust out his manly chest and offered to hold the dog in his arms. It seemed a harmless courtesy. Victor, blocked a little further down the aisle, pushed his way back up with his elbows until he was in better position. Neither of the two had changed that much. They were united in one of those friendships based on distrust. Victor felt for Enriquito a very common sort of envy, the kind provoked by someone in whom you see your own defects, but who has been luckier in life. For his part, Enriquito, with his degree, a profession, and a good salary, felt an ugly little jealousy of Victor's successful marriage.

At the Reina/Lealtad stop, a man got on. An extremely skinny black man, who advanced with jerky, unsettled movements. He was wearing a clean and very worn cotton shirt; his ripped-up and shapeless pants were a map of patches on the backside; his shoes had had the worst of it, dusty and falling apart. Beneath his arm he carried one of those mysterious portfolios that contains who knows what, together with a handful of yellowed newspapers. When I run into such a grey-haired black man, I figure he's at least two hundred fifty years old. However, the strangest thing was his face, drawn, hollow cheeks, bloodshot eyes, a brutally flattened nose, and a mouth that gave the rare impression of being raw flesh. I will never forget that mouth, sprawling, the most visible part of the man's face because it just wouldn't stop trembling, opening and closing. Each time it opened, you could see a couple of sad and threadbare teeth.

The black man's getting on the bus was an event, although I couldn't have said in that moment what kind it was. The first voice that you heard was the driver's. He seemed to not be talking to anybody in particular. In reality he was addressing himself to the man:

"Boxers are nothing but a bunch of good-for-nothings."

The black man's reaction was instantaneous. He jumped like a spring:

"That's exactly right," he squealed in a high voice, too quickly.

I was surprised by everybody's laughter. I smiled as well. I thought that I was witnessing a joke that had been repeated a thousand times. I couldn't have suspected what would come later.

Another man chimed in, "Kid Gavilán knocked you out."

The black man started to jerk his arms spasmodically, and a kind of screech came out of that mouth.

"That's not true."

All of a sudden, I recognized Victor's voice.

"Stop telling fairy tales. Kid Gavilán almost killed you," and he let loose a rough belly laugh, for the benefit of the young ladies with the poodle.

The black man seemed on the verge of tears.

"Liar! Kid Gavilán, it was *me* who knocked *him* out."

Victor returned to the assault.

"Don't start with that, Kid Bururú. Dead men tell no tales."

The man that Victor had called Kid Bururú moved into fighting stance, and the agitation on the bus grew. I looked around me in amazement: wasn't anyone going to stop this?

We crossed Galiano St. and the traffic was horrible. Sweat and grime had discomposed the passengers' faces, rushed, perturbed, as they traveled on the number 19. From the sidewalk somebody yelled a greeting, the poodle surprisingly started to bark, you could hear a siren in the distance. There was a moment of intense uproar, and at the same time, of calm. Kid Bururú managed to sit down on the seat over the back wheel. He had his head between his knees and the look of a boxer who is in his corner waiting for the bell.

It was then that I heard Enriquito's voice saying:

"Kid Gavilán took your wife away."

Kid Bururú was shook by a lightning bolt. He abandoned his seat and tried to move up through the aisle. The riders' faces were no longer quite so all smiles. It was going too far. There was a grumble of disapproval. Although now nothing could hold back Enriquito who, from his seat, repeated like a chorus, "Kid Gavilán took your wife away." And then he added:

"Kid Bururú, you're not a man."

The black man threw himself on Enriquito and threw a left jab to the chin that struck nothing but air. The girls with the poodle coyly cried out once or twice. Victor butted in, and after this minor skirmish they threw him bodily off the bus, at the stop of the Park of Brotherhood. There Kid Bururú stayed, moving one of his pathetic fists, as he kept the other one defensively at the level of his hip, in a position that must remind him of his old glories in the ring.

I closed my eyes because I thought I was going to faint. I reproached myself for my passivity, my silence. And here I asked myself another official question: Does it have to be inevitable that time beats us down?

I looked up, as Victor and Enriquito were stepping down from the bus, together with the young women and the poodle. They were still laughing.

The 19 turned the corner toward Port Avenue and began to empty out. When I least expected it, I caught the smell of gas and rotten planks, and I heard the cushhh, cushhh of the waves that were slapping up against the seawall of the Malecón. The bay was on my right, which was why I had chosen this seat. I had met Marcelo at Casablanca and we had gotten onto a number 19 bus then too. But not even this memory, the best one on my list, could wipe away the image of Kid Bururú.

That afternoon there was a party at my house. The guests were Marcelo and the children. After the feast and the cake, Marcelo asked me:

"And did you end up running into any cannibals?"

I scratched my nose to stall for a minute and said:

"Yes, at least two. I also traveled a lot, much farther than Mars. And I composed an ode to Kid Bururú."

"To who?"

"To Kid Bururú. You have to ride the bus if you want to meet him."

Translated by Sara E. Cooper

PROPHET OF DOOM

The gold bracelet in the jewelry box glows like a sibylline ray in the darkness. A more affected-sounding sentence, impossible. However, it was fascinating to squint and blur the tiny little links, reposing innocently on the black velvet of the case. Good lord! How the charm shined, just like the eyes of Babalao Flores that early morning when they appeared to Zenobia while she was on guard duty for the Committee.[16] It was just past one a.m. and there wasn't a soul in the street. At least that was how it seemed, damn.

Zoilita, the neighbor in back, had just gone into her house looking for a little coffee, and Zenobia took advantage of the opportunity to sit down on the wall next to the front door. A wrought-iron gate creaked with its rusty clattering behind her. A cat was meowing in the distance. The commonplace setting, of course, the most logical thing that could have happened, taking into consideration the event that was about to take place. In the middle of the dark of night, as if floating in an invisible liquid, Zenobia saw the eyes of Babalao Flores. Listen up: only the eyes.

Zenobia, to tell the truth, had never demonstrated any gift for the occult or for sorcery up until that moment. Besides, all that rigmarole required a lot of effort and she just wasn't up to it. She'd been like that since she was a little girl; even moving her mouth to chew wore her out. Her mother had never tired of badgering her about it, not even at her dying moment, on the operating table, honey, at this rate you'll never amount to anything.

Life hadn't stopped being unlucky for Zenobia. Now she had before her the eyes of Babalao Flores hanging on an untouchable line. She was too shocked to be scared. Besides, what evil could they do to her, faithful Zenobia, believing Zenobia, obedient Zenobia? Maybe

---

[16] A Babalao is an authority figure in Afro-Cuban religions, similar to a shaman.

they were a sign that, finally, her luck was going to change. Be that as it may, she didn't plan to mention anything about it to Zoilita. She was capable of advertising Babalao Flores's appearance through the entire neighborhood, turning Zenobia overnight into everyone's laughing stock. No way, girl. When Zoilita came back with the jar of coffee, Zenobia merely allowed herself to introduce the topic of conversation.

"How long has it been since Babalao Flores died, Zoilita?"

"Uuuuh!" Zoilita confirmed with a gesture that gave the impression that she was swatting a fly, but in slow motion. With that, she indicated that it was too long ago to remember. And above all, that it was an annoying topic.

"It hasn't been that long."

Zoilita interrupted her:

"Praise, girl, don't even remind me of that low-life."

Low-life seemed rude, not in keeping with her own image of Babalao Flores. She tried to change the topic of discussion, but it didn't go very well:

"Your husband has turned out so good, Zoilita! You've really been lucky."

"What do you mean lucky, girl?"

Zenobia had missed the mark. She tried to explain:

"The wheel of fortune, Zoilita. Destiny favors some, and others..." the suspension dot, dot, dots also kept floating around in the middle of the night; however, all of them seemed to close ranks around Zenobia.

"What the hell do you mean destiny! Listen to what I'm telling you, people have the fate that they make for themselves," unceremoniously Zoilita waved her index finger in Zenobia's direction and added categorically: "Everything else is bullshit, pretexts, rationalizations, bats in the belfry."

Zenobia shrugged her shoulders and didn't press the point. She looked discreetly towards the corner where seconds earlier the eyes had been hanging. Just the eyes of Babalao Flores, unmistakably. But now there wasn't a trace left of the vision.

It was after that night that Zenobia began to hear very strange phrases. Without a doubt they were an announcement, an omen, a complaint, who knows what. Putting her to the test. How long is this going to last? Zenobia herself said that she had spent her whole life being tested. No luck with men, no job that had lasted, Zenobia's existence had been A CONSTANT PROPHECY OF DOOM. Hail Mary, with the appearance of those eyes maybe at last her luck was changing.

Something was going to happen. First, the eyes, like hanging from an ethereal clothesline, the breath of the Spirit manifesting itself no less when she was on guard duty for the committee and later, at all hours, without prior notice, the appearance of those twisted, pompous phrases full of cryptic messages. Can you believe it! First a moment of silence, followed by a whispering in her ears that then got mixed with howling, just like in mystery movies. The murmur almost always brought an order or a piece of advice. Just like the ones that Babalao Flores used to give them when he was alive.

When Zenobia moved to Guanabacoa, the first formal visit she had made was to the house of Babalao Flores. It was a masonry structure like the rest of the houses in the neighborhood. The entire family lived there: blacks, Chinese, mulattos, of all ages. At the front door you could see a set of everyday wrought iron chairs. Hell, they were what you would call downright common. The rest of the house wasn't anything special either. But it was in the backyard where the Master held court. And back there, yes it was different. Very DIFFERENT, right?

Her very good friend Raquel had taken it upon herself to convince Zenobia. She had to go see Babalao Flores, to consult, to take charge of her life, to cast off all that bad luck, girl.

Her first visit to the backyard remained a disturbing memory for Zenobia. Who would have guessed that so many people could fit in there! From the street no one would have imagined it. Man oh man, there had to be at least fifty people back there.

"Let's come back another day," said Zenobia, changing her mind. She hated that feeling of forced quiet, the air of complicity and the emotion as if they were attending an open-air wake. And on top of that, the look that everyone gave anyone who was arriving for the first time. She felt like an intruder, who had sent her there? It would have been better to have stayed in bed with the blinds down, and not have expended so much energy in vain. Zenobia began to long for the quiet shadows of her room, where nobody bothered her, and no one made her feel like someone who stripped away the rights of others, the rights of the ethereal, that is to say.

"No way, my friend," Raquel answered, stubbornly. "It's always like this. Imagine, half the clientele comes from the boondocks and they make appointments up to three months in advance."

An old woman who was cooling herself with an ugly, palm-leaf fan, interjected into the conversation:

"I didn't even sleep last night in order to save my daughter-in-law's place in line."

Zenobia was used to waiting in line. She'd waited in all kinds. But this one. This was the first time she'd waited in line to find out her fortune, her destiny. Getting together with the GREAT BEYOND!"

It wasn't easy to say, but she definitely did say it:

"Who's last in line?"

Raquel's eyes opened wide and she nudged her with her elbow.

"But, girl, you have an appointment."

She whispered in her ear: "I already took care of it. I spoke with my friend who is Babalao Flores's cousin, and they are going to let you go to the head of the line. Having friends is worth something. Don't you think so? Don't even think about it. THAT'S THE WAY IT IS."

Zenobia and Raquel stood next to the fence covered with hibiscus. The backyard was crowded. Someone had placed some little wooden benches, some folding chairs and also two or three boxes that could double as chairs, all over the place. Lying on his back with his legs stretched out on the grass, a man of about sixty was dozing. Next to him was a cage holding a monkey. In the far corner of the backyard was a small windowless wooden hut with a tin roof and one lone door facing east. Zenobia assumed that was where Babalao Flores received his visitors.

Zenobia looked all around the backyard and fixed her gaze on the cage. The monkey had an immaculate appearance. It was lounging on a plastic carpet, sprawled out between the bars, doing nothing. A little later a woman came out of the house carrying a small broom and began to sweep out the cage. The monkey observed the cleaning with indolence and a certain air of superiority. The woman swept up the nutshells, the excrement, and the gnawed seeds and put them in a wastebasket that she took with her towards the house. She reappeared a little later and changed the water in the monkey's bowl. Zenobia could hear the ice cubes as they cascaded like a waterfall into the dish. Finally the woman crossed the yard with a tray. Only then did the monkey acknowledge her presence; the tray was loaded with mangos and some smoking, pointy pieces of something that Zenobia decided must be pumpkin fritters. The monkey barely had to lift a finger to get the exquisite food into its mouth. Zenobia felt something akin to envy. That was one lucky monkey.

Every once in a while a rather Chinese-looking mulatto came out of the hut. Raquel introduced him to her:

"Zenobia, this is Chan Li Po, the Master's assistant."

The man whom Raquel called Chan Li Po with great familiarity grabbed her hand and rubbed it a little. It won't be long, he told them.

Well, they ended up having to wait something like four hours. Zenobia thought it would never end. She was exhausted, disillusioned. The **moment** was never going to arrive. Then, in the space of a second everything happened all at once: a wave of the fragrance of fried plantains floated out of the kitchen, a coconut shot out of Babalao Flores's door and shattered against the concrete a few feet from the sleeping man, who awoke with a start. Pieces of shell ricocheted onto the grass, looks crossed each other with something like fear, and in the middle of all that the monkey started to masturbate. Zenobia couldn't forgive herself for the materialist, sacrilegious thought that crossed her mind at that crucial moment: man, without a doubt is descended from the monkey.

Immediately she tried to take back the idea, the evolutionist one, you understand, that clashed totally with the ambience of Babalao Flores's backyard.

"It's a question of logistics. The bull couldn't…"

Raquel looked at her incomprehensibly. But Zenobia couldn't continue reflecting because at her side was the Chinese mulatto, the mysterious Chan Li Po, urging her with some little nudges at her waist to go inside the wooden hut.

Zenobia thought that her life was going to improve from that day on. With the help of Babalao Flores all kinds of new roads would be opened up to her. Raquel had known him for years and was one of his devotees.

"Imagine how I prospered with Alfredo thanks to the Master." Raquel told her about how she had met Alfredo, who was wandering around Pajarito Street, dying of hunger, not taking advantage of his six feet, that droopy mustache like Cantinflas and without a cent to his name. Raquel decided to take charge of the situation, she dressed him decently, she paid for his studies and she didn't give him a moment's peace until he earned a civil engineering degree. In those days there was hardly anybody in Cuba who knew anything about that. When the Americans left, Alfredo became a key player within the firm. He worked like a lunatic, that's the plain and simple truth, girl. They lived high on the hog. And what do you think. At that moment Babalao Flores began to act.

The first job that the Master did for Raquel had to do with the Fiat. Do you know what it's like to have a car and to not have to squeeze like sardines into those buses? Well the most important thing is to have faith. That's what I believe. After only fifteen days of going to Babalao Flores, the firm gave Alfredo a company car.

"You don't say!" marveled Zenobia. And her admiration for the Master went up a few more notches.

Then came the matter of the trips. Babalao Flores predicted to Raquel that progress over distances and the removal of obstacles from one's path required a special maneuver. Chan Li Po had specified that the task would cost fifty-seven pesos. Whatever, answered Raquel. If the gods decree it, one must obey. Raquel was determined to do whatever it would take. But, girl, without letting Alfredo find out about it.

From then on, Raquel was tortured by new problems. Having a good-looking husband with a car is a curse. The unknown woman who frequently appeared in the shells[17] filled her with tremendous uneasiness. She began to spy on Alfredo, to smell his handkerchiefs, to turn his pockets inside out, to read his calendar. She couldn't go on living like that. Raquel told Zenobia how, following the advice of Babalao Flores, she had prepared a disgusting concoction, what else could she do? With honey, menstrual blood, two cloves of garlic, and a half-smoked cigar. I can't even begin to tell you what it smelled like, it made you want to puke, girl. She kept the potion hidden under their bed for three months. If Alfredo had found out, he would have killed her. But Raquel was determined to eliminate the unknown woman and that guy who appeared on horseback[18] whose intentions were definitely not good. Surely he was Alfredo's boss, an extremist, a guy who was trying too hard to get ahead. Who did he think he was?

Not an easy job, Babalao Flores had responded. Money is no object. Raquel drew the sign on a piece of cardboard, three crossed arrows with six points, the spell that would bring harm to her enemy.

"I went to Alfredo's office and I put it in a drawer. What do you think about that?"

"Great." Zenobia barely had time to answer.

"But you know how IT goes," Raquel lowered her voice, but the capital letters resonated throughout the room.

No, Zenobia did not know.

---

[17] Cowry shells that are read and used to predict the future.
[18] These are characters that appeared in the reading of the shells.

"Yes, girl. One has to help providence out a little. Go to the beauty parlor, update your wardrobe, replay the mushy parts of your first years of marriage. You know how it goes. The *coup de grace* was the syrup that I gave Alfredo every morning on his breakfast."

That was that. The unknown woman didn't reappear in the shells, and barely two months later they canned Alfredo's boss. Not a week after they got rid of him, can you believe it, they notified Alfredo that they were sending him to Portugal.

"That's how I got my first pair of foreign shoes, my friend."

This Babalao Flores is incredible.

Although, truth be told, the days passed and Zenobia's life didn't get any better. Chan Li Po slipped his hand through her arm and recommended she be patient, very patient. Chan Li Po had the skin and features of a Chinese mulatto, but Babalao Flores was a very black, black man. His grandmother had been Kimbisa[19] and in one of those strange twists of fate had ended up in Guanabacoa, where she formed a family with a Chinese man from Canton and forgot forever about the Matanzas congregation. Now her grandson was resurrecting the tradition. But at times in the backyard you could hear the scattered laughter of Babalao Flores's great-grandchildren who would come home from school, stick their heads in the backyard and laugh mockingly. They would throw little rocks at the monkey cage and then run away. They didn't respect anything, girl. Zenobia saw them go by as if through a fog while she was waiting for her turn to consult with the Master, to face the very starched white shirt, the silver bangles on his muscular wrist, the bracelet of bright colors around the skin of an ankle that was too gray from circulatory problems. The earthly always alternating with the spiritual, but, oh, the soul overflowing with grace and purity. Zenobia's chastity at the age of forty-eight. Too much virginity, Zenobia told herself, couldn't the Master do something for her? However, what value did the perishable flesh possess? Keep yourself safe from rumors and essences. Always had

---

[19] Kimbisa is one of the Afro-Cuban religions.

some ancient saying: Beware, the day of the devil, the night of Endoki, don't let anyone lay eyes upon you on Tuesday.

Just before he died, Babalao Flores ordered Zenobia to learn to talk with the secret drum. That was a man's domain, but the Father had revealed to him that only in this way could she confront the evil forces. Envy, misplaced ambition, evil tongues. Rubbing the Kinfuiti drum hidden under her bed. That bed that was too big for Zenobia.

Raquel thought it was a great remedy. You pay attention to the Master, girl, it was thanks to the bellowing of the Kinfuiti drum that I managed to get Alfredo chosen as an Advanced Worker.[20] Look, what good fortune, Raquel announced, opening wide the doors of her sideboard before Zenobia's admiring eyes. That one is Las Mercedes,[21] who looks out for me.

And when will it be her turn? It was around then that Zenobia was really impressed by the time that they went together to a calling up of the saints in La Lisa. Before leaving her friend's house, Raquel rubbed a chocolate paste on the soles of their shoes. In order to take good steps, she told her. Raquel knew a whole lot about occult powers, hidden mysteries, mysticism, omens, and witches Sabbaths, Cuban style. And she introduced her to all that. They arrived very early to the ritual. In the living room of the house they had set up an altar to Saint Barbara, who is the same as Changó, the troublemaking, womanizing, red god who was always ready to cause problems. Along the width of the floor the libations in his honor were accumulating: sweets, demijohns of brandy, pots of beans, candies, plates of yucca with *mojo* sauce, the offerings to the saint to keep him happy. Raquel squatted and added a bar of caramel-coated peanuts. In the other room an old, super old man with a red handkerchief rolled around his ancient neck was balanced on a stool; over his head was nailed a varnished shelf displaying a rag doll, several necklaces, a glass of water, a Czech crystal goblet full of

---

[20] Advanced Worker is an honorary designation, bestowed for having performed in an exemplary manner.
[21] The Virgin of the Mercies, and the Catholic equivalent of the African saint, Obbatala.

black pennies, and a copper amulet. To the left of the old man, on the wall, was hanging a glass-covered engraving of a gigantic eye that was looking straight at Zenobia, or at least that's the sensation it gave her. Half an hour later, not one more person would have fit in the place. The bodies were crammed together, oozing sweat and the acrid smell of alcohol mixed with talcum powder and cheap cologne; a purring from the interior announced that the ceremony was about to begin, the sound grew rhythmically until the majority of those in attendance were undulating in an up and down motion in time with the music. An old woman dressed in white shoes, robe, and cap went to the center and continued dancing on her own with a calm yet passionate mobility, accentuating her steps with a yellow scarf. Suddenly a blue-eyed, mulatto little boy with an "it wasn't me" look on his face appeared in the circle and let out a guttural scream. Raquel pressed her lips against the nape of Zenobia's neck and explained to her that Yemayá, the Mother of Water, had just entered the little boy. And suddenly, the insipid face of that little boy began to glow, look at that, the little fellow panting as if he were having an attack, the little guy leaping around in a hair-raising manner until he came to a stop right in front of Zenobia, she became incarnate for you, girl, and with a super affected voice he told her that she had a great light around her, and that she need not worry any more, the goddess was transmitting that all her roads were open.

But not a chance.

Then Babalao Flores died, and after a while Zenobia began to hear the twisted phrases, with that howling that made her hair stand on end.

How those gold links shone in the jewelry box. It was all the work of Babalao Flores. When Zenobia heard that imperious whispering next to her right ear, she didn't doubt for an instant before putting her hand into Romelia's jewelry box and grabbing the bracelet. Babalao Flores's order is her command. The gods rule. Besides, what did Romelia want the bracelet for, if she never went out anywhere? The gold chain shines like alabaster on your breast, chosen one of the spirits, may you sleep peacefully, may your stagnation end. Bless you a thousand times. I wonder what the Master meant by all that? The dead out there with their wisdom. She had obeyed him promptly and now Romelia's gold bracelet was resting inside her velvet-lined jewelry box. Safe and sound, in Zenobia's sideboard. Of course, that was where it needed to be.

Would he be pleased? Satisfied with her? The master perhaps finally would be happy with his pupil. What was Babalao Flores going to ask her to do next, so that finally Zenobia's roads would open up for her?

Just a few days after the incident with the bracelet, once again the moment of silence, the buzzing and another one of those complicated phrases came to Zenobia. The more you try to avoid trouble, the more it has a way of finding you. Let it go. Babalao Flores himself came up with the solution: appease the immortal power until you're totally exhausted. A complicated, excessive order. If only Raquel were with her to give her strength. But no. At this late date Zenobia had to act alone.

Zenobia opened the door of the wooden hut and tried to let her eyes adjust to the darkness. Chan Li Po was waiting in that unstarched, hard old bed that had been presiding over one of the corners, since the far-off times of Babalao Flores. Now the Chinese mulatto occupied it, impassive, his extended gaze a little anxious while Zenobia unbuttoned her dress. Chan Li Po didn't say a word and Zenobia didn't dare to speak about Babalao Flores, not even when in the semi-darkness of the dawn she saw his eyes again, dying from laughter, asking for more and more.

Translated by Victoria L. McCard

THE BLIND BUFFALO

For Miguel Carralero and Iván Garcia

I had been carrying around this coin everywhere I went for a long time—it was more than just a good-luck charm. In a little bitty town like this one everybody knows everybody else's business, but my secret was very well kept. I feel I need to confess something right off: I started playing the innocent at a very young age. And I was good, let me tell you. Because the first ideas that I just couldn't wrap my head around were finding that coin and seeing the sad face of my town.

Those days if somebody started talking about anywhere far away, they'd probably end up mentioning any number of houses: a house in the boondocks, a house in the middle of nowhere, a house all the way to hell and back, or even the devil's own house. I'm not going to spend any time on the possible origins of these abodes, but speaking of the devil, you'd also hear people refer to remote locations as the devil's playground. Or sometimes they'd compare them to some fictional geographic zone like The-Ends-of-the-Earth or Timbuktu. But what you always heard in those years I'm talking about was people calling my town, Esmeralda, the asshole of the world.

I agree it doesn't qualify as a pretty or poetic phrase, but it has the advantage of being graphic enough to get across the exact sensation that would crush you as you traveled the mile after mile of monotonous sugar cane fields that separated Esmeralda from the district capital. Not to mention the chimerical road that linked my town to the resplendent Havana, barely glimpsed in dreams and newspaper clippings.

Esmeralda was named after a green jewel, although during periods of drought it was merely dusty and, in my humble opinion, a true nothings-ville. The only spot that allowed a little light into our dark routine was the railway station. The red tiles of its roof neatly framed a platform that I was sure I had seen in more than eighteen cowboy-and-

Indians movies. The platform even came with tumbleweeds dragged around by the wind. To top this off, the station was called Woodin, a name that fit perfectly with the image of the stagecoach, the saloon, and the sign rusted by the prairie air which has been burned into memory thanks to Metro Goldwyn Mayer. And despite the shortage of Hollywood emotions at Woodin, it was nonetheless the magic landscape where any novelty arrived. My parents' house was barely fifty yards from the train station, separated from it by a mom and pop store with ostentatious Doric, Ionic, or maybe Corinthian columns—I never could find out which. So my favorite and not very original entertainment was to keep watch over the arrivals and departures of the trains, or of anything else capable of moving on those tracks.

The neighborhood knew me well. I was the only daughter of the always broke notary, also nothing out of the ordinary, you might say. A common enough little girl, tending toward awkward movements and crooked ribbons, without dazzling grades or reports of poor conduct. Because of my reputation as a mousey homebody, my sneakiness with the coin didn't raise any eyebrows. I, of course, and let me spell it out for you, believed that I was really out of this world. Seriously.

When I say out of this world, I don't mean merely exceptional, or more intelligent that the rest, but moreover, quite literally, from another planet. No comments from the peanut gallery, thank you.

That belief could be blamed partly on the radio broadcasts my mother and I listened to with eager loyalty at noon or nightfall, sitting on the porch as we awaited the mail or newspaper that would come from the aforementioned Woodin station, and partly on the delusions of grandeur I had acquired since my father had begun to let me paw through his eclectic library. There I rummaged, morning, afternoon, and evening, without restriction of any kind. In my incursions through bookshelves, glass cabinets, credenzas, corner cupboards, and armoires I was just as enthralled by the epic novels—shelved with complete disregard to logic, related only by the shared dust and humidity—as by those enormous tomes with worn-out spines and sundry contents that went by the title of *encyclopedia*. Not to mention the colossal pile of full-color magazines in some strange language, bursting with illustrations from all over the planet Earth, just what I was dying to see first-hand, from one end to the other. The ritual scene was completed by a globe, faded and bulging in inappropriate places, an inkwell with a faun's head, and a tiny bronze figure of Don Quixote, trophies from my father's career at the university.

I think that the poor notary Mr. Balboa, whose Christian name was Wilde—witty joke or historical mania of my grandfather's which made my father's life no walk in the park—I repeat, I believe that my poor notary had no inkling of any danger lurking in the dull little girl I pretended to be. By then I had realized the obvious necessity of keeping my planetary condition under wraps. If the others had discovered who I really was, all would have been lost. They would have sent me without a second thought to heaven knows what dungeon, or worse, to a convent where they could lock up anybody who dared to interrupt the regularity of Esmeralda. At least something like that had happened to a third cousin of mine after some love affair with a stranger, maybe a Martian.

My intuition warned me that what is different is usually punished. And here I was, nothing less than a native of another planet.

Another fact to keep in mind: all kinds of people ended up dropping by my house. Be it for professional consultations, because of its proximity to Woodin, or on account of my mother's coffee, the rocking chairs on our front porch enjoyed a virtual parade of heterogeneous behinds. And you had to hear them talk. One of them, I no longer remember who, and it doesn't matter anymore anyway, confided to me a certain fact. It concerned the existence of a five-cent coin, a so-called *nickel,* with the silhouette of a buffalo, nothing all that special. What nobody else knew was that you had to look for a surviving coin from a particular minting, where the buffalo was lying on its side, still your everyday nickel, but from 1914. And then came the best part: it was worth a million dollars.

My confidante's persuasive and mysterious tone, coupled with the historical data related to the First World War, gave the story a convincing ring of truth. A million dollars! The mere mention of the amount made me dizzy. It was an astronomical amount and in my fantasies was along the lines of the light-years of distance between the stars. Of course, even Havana seemed light-years away back then. None of my dreams had dared to stretch so far. I looked toward the station, the engine whistled, and the wagons began to move slowly; as I counted the railway's crossties, crosspieces, wooden rollers, girders, and rafters to infinity, I compulsively calculated everything I would be able to do with a coin like that. And I had to stop, sit down, think of something else, let my mind wander, because I would get so light-headed.

One day that seemed like any other, the kind that only later will be drilled into your memory, a bolt of lightening in a clear sky of identical days, Mom sent me to that store with Doric, Ionic, or Corinthian columns to buy something trivial, like twenty-five cents worth of capers. I paid with a dollar bill and, receiving my change, I spread it out in my hand like always, expecting nothing. But...Ladies and Gentlemen! There was my coin! The buffalo minted in 1914 had fallen into my power. I don't have to tell you how that breathtaking apparition amidst the dirty quarters seemed to me to be a sign of the high places I was destined to go—ribbons, dirty fingernails, and scraped knees notwithstanding.

I was trembling by the time I got home, looking like a drowned rat, and my mother mistook my frenzy for some malarial fevers that were going around. She sounded the infectious alarm, and I was thrown under five blankets with a hot-water bottle tucked at my feet. After drinking a disgusting concoction I fell asleep, the coin still in my hand, shiny from the polishing of time and the rubbing of countless fingers.

Anxious and half-awake during the entire night, I perceived my mother as a blurry figure that would approach and recede from my bed, without succeeding in penetrating the ineffable haze that surrounded me. I had finally been blessed with my first message from that other—superior—world. To tell the truth, my imagination confused that other world with the tales of Havana I had heard repeated so often.

Under the morning light, since I had no fever or other symptoms, my mother declared me cured. But as I still was acting strangely, she kept a close eye on me, watching me with a curiosity that at any moment could turn into a spanking. Over the course of that day, I went back and forth three or four times as to whether or not I should share my secret with her. But I decided to let Mom keep her innocence. I mean, how could she have dealt with the unexpected news that her daughter was the sole owner of a million dollars?

When I finally managed to be alone, once again I checked the date stamped along the edge of the coin. I confirmed with relief that nothing had changed, and my buffalo was still there, with its Olympic profile, an omen that could slip into any crevice etched away by some termite, easily lost for another forty years. So now I would have to find it a secure hiding place. A dedicated reader of detective stories, I knew that the best place to hide anything was in plain sight. So instead of burying my coin in traditional pirate fashion, or building a secret Gothic drawer in my dresser, I wrapped it in pink tissue paper and put it at the bottom of my box of baby powder. The buffalo deserved any pampering I could think of, as he was the keeper of my fortunes—and my ticket out of Esmeralda!

Every night, before going to sleep, I dusted off the coin, shined it up, sometimes holding it against my forehead, sometimes balancing it on my thumb. By handling it so much I became convinced that the buffalo on my coin was not ignorant of what was happening. I addressed long monologues to him, although his huge head never deigned to turn around and look at me. Because of this I got it into my head that he must be blind. If he hadn't been, he would have had more than enough time to recognize me, his owner. His mistress.

In spite of my protector's blindness, a change had taken place deep in my soul. I stopped sharing my mother's financial worries and my father's anxieties about my future. I possessed the truth. Besides, my blind buffalo would always be there to get me out of trouble when I needed him to.

After that I ignored the radio shows and stopped paying any attention to the previously fascinating Woodin. Every time I had the chance, I locked myself in my room to fabricate lists of all the things I was going to do with the blind buffalo's help. I might as well confess honestly, with a tinge of embarrassment, that in all my plans there was not a single act of charity. I wasn't going to donate my million to orphaned children or to found a ladies' association to combat polio; I didn't even think of buying a marble bench for Esmeralda's park, to perpetuate the Balboa name. Nothing of the sort. My dreams came from the books I had read, full of adventures and exploring. And they were closely connected to the mountain of magazines, the thick mildewed novels, the encyclopedia, and the faded globe of the Earth. My blind buffalo would take me to the Islam of *Arabian Nights;* to Casablanca; to a medieval castle, especially to the one at Mont Saint-Michel at low tide; with it I would roam the Winter Palace, Baker Street, and my grandparents' ancestral lands in Galicia. Then I would have my picture taken next to the flag at the North Pole and beside a dog sled in the Klondike. I would do carnival in Rio de Janeiro; I would cross the Sahara on camelback, and later I would travel to Tahiti on a raft like the *Kon-Tiki*. There would have to be a lion hunt in Africa and, of course, another for the white whale; I would feed the doves in the Piazza de San Marco and listen to the thunder of Niagara Falls. I would follow Marco Polo's route, float down the Amazon, and find El Dorado; I would climb the pyramid of Teotihuacán and see who knows how many of the Seven Wonders of the World. I would visit, as if all that weren't enough, Tom Sawyer's cave and Jean Christophe's Parisian attic. This may seem like an ambitious plan, but a million was a million. My blind buffalo could do anything.

You may well imagine that as more time went by I was less and less inclined to reveal to my relatives that they had a millionaire in the family. I didn't want to get Esmeralda all up in arms, and I wasn't ready for them to start treating me, at such a tender age, with the reverence I deserved. There would be time enough for that. I didn't want to embarrass my parents or to interrupt the placid flow of life in Esmeralda.

So it was something else that happened around that time that shattered our small-town tranquility.

Across the street from my house there lived quite the clan of town society. As far as I could make out, the family included an indeterminate number of old people, aunts and uncles, grandparents, in-laws, and to top it off two unmarried young ladies. My two neighbors were not going to be twenty-something much longer, and to me they seemed to be a pair of old maids, not only because thirty seemed a long way off to a snot-nosed girl not even ten, but also because of their convent-like clothes, their immense eyes locked behind the tyrannical patriarchal iron gates, and their measured steps as they made their way to Mass every Sunday, the only walk the Misses Saínz were allowed to take. Their names were Silvina and María Isabel, although it was never very clear to me which one was which.

Well literally overnight the two sisters were seized by a whim to take off for Havana. A rumor sizzled like gunpowder all through Esmeralda. The scandal exploded with a force inversely proportionate to the neighborhood's usually sleepy routine. They had never seen such a flaunting of the rules governing feminine behavior, unmarried girls raising Cain, as the saying goes, with no one to stop them! In vain were the tears of their aunts and cousins-in-law, the fatherly indignation, the moral discombobulating of in-laws and grandparents. The same went for the "no dowry" threat hanging over their virginal heads. It was a disgrace, my parents told each other in whispers over lunch. A horrible desecration of our most sacred traditions. Those Misses Saínz were most definitely going too far!

The departure was announced, as was the "We-said-we-were-going-and-that's-final," the "over-my-dead-body," and the "don't-darken-this-door-again," and on the afternoon of reckoning, a Holy

Friday, they left dressed in their best, wearing the cutest little hats and carrying coffee-colored antediluvian suitcases, though they were a bit cowed under the disapproving gaze of the entire town of Esmeralda, who had gathered to punish the pair of reprobates with their glares. The two walked the fifty meters that separated the patriarchal gates from the railway station where once a week the train would stop on its way to Santa Clara, where it connected with the longed-for convoy going to Havana, the mysterious and, so people said, depraved Havana.

I, too, entrenched myself at our front window and watched them go by. My heart accompanied them in their daring walk, and amidst all the pleas for their good fortune that flew through my mind in that moment, not the least of them was a demand that the blind buffalo give them a bit of luck. Boy what they could have done with at least a fifth of my million dollars. The idea occurred to me as they climbed into the train car, leaving on the platform a mob of little kids and a few adults with sullen and pained expressions. The engine whistled—what could I do! I ran like a meteor with my coin in hand, reached the edge of the platform and there encountered María Isabel's (or was it Silvina's) yearning gaze escaping through the window, setting out for a faraway place. Then I heard a shriek, a sort of sharp trill, as if something had broken into a thousand pieces. Two seconds later they were descending from the train, Silvina—or perhaps it was María Isabel—with her head bowed over her chest, while her sister held those avid eyes fixed on some distant point.

In front of the town's astonished eyes they retraced the few steps that returned them to their house. When the gate closed behind Silvina and María Isabel I suffered, for the first time in my life, an unbearable feeling of frustration. Of course back then I didn't use such words, I barely managed to think that they had grabbed something very valuable right out of my hands, and I judged them harshly, with all the cruelty of childhood, those poor girls who couldn't break away from all of that, that which for me could be summarized in one word: Esmeralda.

The same evening, with my coin hidden under my pajamas and

next to my heart, I made a decision: I would get to Havana no matter whose dead body it was over, I would study archaeology, and I would become famous. The blind buffalo was in my corner.

The uproar surrounding Silvina and María Isabel didn't stop there. From that dark day forward, the two sisters returned to the station every Friday of each and every week, with their two sweet hats, little by little getting frayed, and their set of coffee-colored suitcases, scuffed from so much back and forth. They would climb into the train car, settle on their seats—always the same seats—and wait there until the engine whistled before descending and withdrawing behind the gates of home. Week after week, which turned into month after month. At first people took it very seriously, then a bit later found it amusing, until finally only indifference permeated Silvina and María Isabel's weekly journey, a voyage with its touch of Sisyphus, a bit of Tantalus, and a fair share of who-in-the-hell-knows.

The years went by and nothing changed in my neighbors' lives, although history shifted, in terms of little things and big. My time had come too, in the shape of a scholarship to an institute for know-it-all children. It was finally my turn to climb onto the train heading for Havana! By then I hardly ever thought of the blind buffalo, or of that afternoon when my eyes hit María Isabel's (or was it Silvina's) hungry gaze, desperate to flee through the window of that train car sitting at Woodin Station. I had also for the most part forgotten my otherworldly origins.

As I hugged my parents goodbye, I looked without sadness toward the gloomy hallways of my house, knowing that this was my last day in Esmeralda. But something happened that clouded my happiness. As I was climbing onto the train I bumped into Silvina (or was it María Isabel); her head was bowed and her vague glance was the dust of a long drought. She murmured only a few words: "never amount to anything." The phrase, not addressed to me, not to anyone, jolted my heart, and I took it as if it had been a second message from that other world.

The story that follows is practically cliché, as often as it happens.

I studied with dedication and a vague recollection of the belief that I was one of the chosen of the universe. My grades were always excellent, and the prizes, honors, and promotions accumulated. I continued to play the innocent, but in my own defense let me say that I wasn't completely lacking in talent, and I was hard working and easy going. I have to say that the times were very generous to me, and every so often I would think of that country bumpkin from Esmeralda, now a Ph.D., chief of a technical department, with a grand two-story house in Miramar and a bunch of other things that are beside the point.

Once in a while, in a bout of cleaning or searching through mounds of papers, I would run into my blind buffalo, relegated to the faraway realm of childish nonsense, stripped forever of that limitless power bestowed on it back then, by the girl I once was. Its nature clashed with the practical, utilitarian objects on my desk, but for some reason I never could throw it away, and so it would move from one side to the other of my junk drawer.

Last week I attended a conference in the city of Camaguey. As I drove back I couldn't resist the urge to take a detour and go through Esmeralda. A lot had changed in twenty years. To make a long story short, the expected chaos of progress. My house was gone, but the indomitable general store with its Doric, Ionic, or Corinthian columns was still there. The wood and tile railway station, the melodious Woodin, had given way to a cement building. Without giving myself the time to think twice, I set off toward the Saínz sisters' gate.

I wasn't all that surprised when I made out Silvina and María Isabel, seated in their cedar rockers behind the gates, one of them with her head drooping over her black muslin décolletage, the other with that same searching gaze, two sisters captured for posterity as in a daguerreotype.

Pretending a self-confidence that I was very far from feeling, I pushed open the gate and sat down without permission on the portico step of the Misses Saínz's rotting veranda. I didn't mention the Balboa name, or tell stories from the twenty years that had made their mark on the rest of the world; in truth I barely said a word in the conversation that for more than five hours I unraveled with María Isabel, or was it Silvina, while her sister followed the progress of the chat with her head listlessly resting on her chest, sadly marking the rhythm of the words with a slight bob to the right or to the left, defeated.

For the first time in oh so many months I was oblivious to being in a hurry and on a schedule. María Isabel's tempered voice (I suppose it was she) related in spirited tones the globetrotting exploits of an ardent wanderer, the escapades of a traveler versed in all the routes, pathways and oceans of the earth's globe. From her chatter, which sounded so natural to my ears, flowed a whirlwind of tales told with an extravagance and passion that wasn't excavated from any encyclopedia, or even from that mountain of geographic magazines. Her yearning gaze seemed to have come back from the farthest corners of the earth, and an elemental happiness sprung from the pores of that traveler stranded in her nunnery in Esmeralda.

During my drive back I wondered if they still continued to take their places in the train car, week after week, and then suddenly I realized that it didn't matter any more.

When I got home I had time for two other thoughts. This is one of them: on the steps of a railway car, twenty years before, I hadn't been able to grasp the real message. And this was the other: I had spent those years like a bull in the china shop of life, without even seeing it. At a scientific conference in Canada, I didn't hear the Falls; when I visited Paris I forgot Jean Christophe's attic; in Leningrad, my schedule didn't let me visit the Winter Palace. I chose my car over rafts, dogsleds, and camels; as far as the pigeons at the Piazza de San Marco go, I must confess that it was all I could do to keep them from staining my new dress. I went to my junk drawer, and the poor blind buffalo couldn't avoid hearing a few four-letter words I have no intention of repeating here, and which I addressed, as you may well guess, to myself. Then his huge head turned towards me and he looked at me with eyes open wide. It must be early signs of senility.

Translated by Lizabeth Paravisini-Gebert and Sara E. Cooper

NO CALL OF THE WILD

The dog had stayed behind. Maybe he wasn't called Buck, although that one didn't ever read the newspaper either, so he didn't suspect anything. The house was closed up and the garden stopped behind a two meter-high fence, covered with stretches of vine. The dog was standing at the doorway, vigilant, with his ears perked, waiting. From the street you couldn't really make him out. From the little windows of the street bus you could see not just the dog, but also the official seal that secured the house.

The dog was white, with a few dark patches on his chest and sides, short-haired and shiny, well cared for. For the first few days he stayed at attention on all four paws, sure and arrogant. He didn't sniff the wind nor did he move, he simply waited. The house was one of the old-fashioned ones in the Vedado neighborhood. Nevertheless, the garden was still green, and the foliage seemed to have been pruned in recent times. The breath of neglect that would take over all of its nicks and crannies had not yet erased the memory of the hands that had attended it.

After a number of days, the dog remained in the same position, just to the side of the front entrance. Without a doubt he didn't want to move, so that he could be the first one to notice the return of the people he identified as having the right to enter the house and take back up their lives, the only life he had ever known. He kept to his spot, with the same proud gaze, sure of himself, although his beautiful coat started to look a little shabby. You might think that he would be getting impatient by now, that he had lost the thrill of the game, that the joke wasn't funny any more.

A week after, the dog was clearly perplexed. What was going on? What could he have done wrong? Why had his owners, his gods, not come back? He stayed standing and staring fixedly toward the exact point where he had seen his family for the last time, but by this time with a certain disquiet and fatigue, and most certainly hungry and thirsty. He didn't care that much, to tell the truth, about the lack of food. Neither did he worry about not being able to get into his favorite cubbyhole, curl up, sigh, and go to sleep with his heart at peace. His entire little brain was concentrating on understanding the reason behind that punishment that he didn't think he deserved.

The dog had never even heard of Buck, so he didn't feel like a hero. He had never seen the snow, or toboggans, or ice fields, or anything like the environs of the Klondike. Nobody had ever hit him with a stick. When he walked through the neighborhood they took him on the most comfortable leashes, which made him feel protected more than anything else, and he hadn't the faintest idea that other dogs like himself could kill each other with their teeth. This was the house where he had always lived, since they brought him there as a puppy. Behind the sealed door were his hideaways, his water bowl and his pan full of food. Although that was the least of it. Why had they abandoned him?

Fifteen days out he was still standing, resigned, like the victim of some incomprehensible mistake. But his exhaustion ended up getting the better of him, and he found himself unable to keep from leaning against the door. His eyes drooped and he dreamed. He dreamed that his family had come back, that the house was full of voices and familiar sounds, the windows were open to let in the morning sun, and he woke up delighted, giving a bark that fell into silence and then into wrenching rage. He felt betrayed, furious, once again it was there, the nightmare of the house closed up, the garden that was drying out as was his own body. No longer did he ask himself what he had done wrong, he only wanted the punishment to end.

After a time, he began to look ragged, although he continued to gaze out at the same spot. His ears sticking up were the last vestige of his alertness of the first few days. His body was gaunt and sunken in, his coat gummy and his stare like glass. His wait was coming to an end, and something akin to pity, to forgiveness, came into the dog's loyal heart. They, his gods, surely knew why they had done it.

Hortensia, Julia's mother, lived on the top floor of the building next to the dog's house. The stairwell didn't have any light bulbs, and Hortensia had started to lose her sight, so she never went out and just sat in her balcony to listen to the sounds of the street. Hortensia, like Buck, didn't read the paper. She would have liked to listen to the radio, to her soap operas, like Julia said, but it had been broken for a hundred years. Patches had kept her company, before she had died. Hortensia would tell her good morning, scold her, and once in a while, tell her everything that weighed on her mind. Patches had made her existence seem almost fun. Hortensia missed her so much, but what could she do about it, if she couldn't even take care of herself anymore, you tell me, how was she going to take care of another dog. Her neighbor who helped her now and then never said much of anything, she had her own troubles, and at least she came to air out the house and to bring her groceries from the store. Hortensia felt bad for bothering her and hated to even ask her to please read to her the letters from her daughter that, from time to time, arrived from Argentina. When Julia would send her one of those packages with soap and her heart medication, Hortensia would give away the soap to the neighbor. She would have liked to hear Julia's voice too, but, blessed Mary Mother of God, you see how expensive those calls to far off places are. And the years went by, and the years kept on passing, hoping for better days to come. Thank heaven that she never ran out of soap or medicine. And, as luck would have it, she was just about blind, so she couldn't make out the dog.

A month after the fact the dog was gone. He hadn't been defeated by the snow storms, or the wolves, or his hunger, but rather the immense sadness that kept him from doing anything but continue guarding the house and waiting, alone, their return.

Translated by Sara E. Cooper

ABOUT THE TRANSLATORS

Dr. Sara E. Cooper (Ph.D. University of Texas, 1999) is Associate Professor at California State University, Chico. She teaches Spanish, Contemporary Latin American, Latina/o and Chicana/o cultural production and Gender/Queer Studies. She is the founder of the Cuban and Cuban Diaspora Cultural Expression Discussion Group of the Modern Language Association and has a special interest in women's experiences in Cuba. She is the editor of *The Ties That Bind: Questioning Family Dynamics and Family Discourse in Hispanic Literature and Film* as well as *Lesbian Images in International Popular Culture* (also a special issue of the *Journal of Lesbian Studies*). She is the translator of *Burnt Honey*—a novel by Chicano Antonio Arreguín Bermúdez and works by Cuban Mirta Yáñez. Her articles and translations appear in several journals and anthologies, including: *Letras femeninas, Chasqui, Confluencia, Cuban Studies, Kunapipi, A Changing Cuba in a Changing World, Cultura y letras cubanas en el siglo XXI, Tortilleras: Hispanic and Latina Lesbian Expression, Journal of Lesbian Studies, Interdisciplinary Literary Studies* and *Challenging Lesbian Norms*. Dr. Cooper currently is working on a book about humor in post-revolutionary Cuba. She may be reached via e-mail at scooper@csuchico.edu.

Leslie Bary is a comparatist working in Spanish American and Luso-Brazilian literatures. Among her publications are a number of articles on modern Peruvian and Brazilian writers, and on 19th and 20th century Latin American culture, in journals such as *Hispania, Latin American Literary Review, Chasqui, Revista de Crítica Literaria Latinoamericana,* and *Twentieth Century/Siglo XX,* and translations of Oswald de Andrade and other modern Brazilian poets. She has also published short stories in *Outlet* (Berkeley, CA) and *Helicopter/Helicoptero* (Eugene, OR), and she has several essays archived online at www.henciclopedia.org.uy. She teaches Latin American literature at the University of Louisiana-Lafayette. She may be reached via e-mail at lbary@louisiana.edu.

Victoria L. McCard (Ph.D. Emory University, 1992) is Professor of Spanish at North Georgia College & State University, in Dahlonega, Georgia, specializing in contemporary Latin American literature. She has lectured on a variety of figures and topics, including the symbiosis of Federico García Lorca and Salvador Dalí, irony in Mirta Yáñez, *jineterismo* in Luis Manuel García, and *choteo* in Pedro Juan Gutiérrez and Nancy Alonso. She has published articles on the subaltern in Julio Cortázar, Pablo Neruda's banquet, literary depictions of *soldaderas* of the Mexican Revolution, and the double life of the *jinetera* in Daína Chaviano. She is currently awaiting publication of an article on approaches to authority in Nancy Alonso. She may be reached via e-mail at vmccard@northgeorgia.edu.

Lizabeth Paravisini-Gebert is Professor of Caribbean and Latin American literature in the Department of Hispanic Studies at Vassar. She received a B.A. from the University of Puerto Rico, and an M.A., an M.Phil, and Ph.D. in Comparative Literature from New York University (1982). She is the author of *Phyllis Shand Allfrey: A Caribbean Life* (Rutgers UP, 1996), *Jamaica Kincaid: A Critical Companion* (Greenwood Press, 1998), and co-author of *Caribbean Women Novelists: An Annotated Bibliography* (Greenwood, 1993) with Olga Torres Seda. She has edited *Sacred Possessions: Vodoun, Santería, Obeah and the Caribbean* (with Margarite Fernández Olmos, Rutgers UP, 1996), Ana Roqué's 1903 novel *Luz y sombra* (University of Puerto Rico Press, 1991), *Green Cane and Juicy Flotsam: Short Stories by Caribbean Women* (with Carmen Esteves, Rutgers UP, 1991), *El placer de la palabra: literatura erótica femenina de América Latina* (with Margarite Fernández Olmos, Editorial Planeta, 1991), its English version, *Pleasure and the Word: Erotic Writings by Latin American Women* (White Pine Press and Plume, 1993), and *Remaking a Lost Harmony: Short Stories from the Hispanic Caribbean* (with Margarite Fernández Olmos, White Pine Press, 1995). She may be reached via e-mail at liparavisini@vassar.edu.

Claudette Williams holds a PhD in Spanish from Stanford University and is currently professor of Hispanic Caribbean literature in the Department of Modern Languages & Literatures at the Mona Campus of the University of the West Indies. Her first book, *Charcoal and Cinnamon: The Politics of Color in Spanish Caribbean Literature* (University Press of Florida, 2000) broke new ground in the study of Caribbean literature and has been referenced internationally in research on gender and racial politics in Latin America and the Caribbean. Her essays have appeared in various international journals such as *Afro-Hispanic Review, Revista Interamericana* and *Contemporary Literary Criticism*. In addition to literary research, Professor Williams has made significant contributions in the field of translation, and her services have been sought internationally for the dissemination of Spanish Caribbean texts to an English-speaking readership in both print and online media. Her recent book entitled *The Devil in the Details: Cuban Antislavery Narrative in the Postmodern Age* was published by the UWI Press in June 2010.

FORTHCOMING FROM CUBANABOOKS IN 2011

Nancy Alonso's *Disconnect*

Nancy Alonso's stories easily cross the Great Blue River, as Hemingway called the Gulf Stream. Looking out toward the sea from Cojímar, where she lives, Alonso seems destined to bridge that divide with stories that resonate with Cubans wherever they live. One of the stories in *Desencuentro* perfectly makes this point as it describes parallel celebrations in Havana and Miami, of the twenty-fifth anniversary of a college preparatory inauguration. Graduates on both shores, independent of each other, decide to celebrate the date. A phone call at the conclusion of the festivities connects the two "disconnected" groups. As the narrator states: "Although they might be separated by the longest ninety miles geographically speaking, they were also the shortest ninety miles."

Friend and mentor, Mirta Yañez, renowned as both literary critic and successful author, was one of the first to recognize Alonso's skills of observation and encouraged her literary path. Since then many have critiqued and described Alonso's fiction. Well-known Cuban writer, María Elena Llana, calls Alonso's latest work "beautiful for its bravery," a work that presents the homoerotic world without veiled allusions and yet never in a tawdry or distasteful fashion. Llana also confirms a characteristic of Alonso's works in general: their intrinsic linkage to the multiple vicissitudes of national life. Cuban-born Carlos Espinosa Domínguez, a professor at Mississippi State, notes Alonso's tendency toward brevity, her connection with Borges—a quote from "The Garden of Forking Paths" at the beginning of *Desencuentro* provides a framework for the collection—and her approach to reality from unexpected angles.

Alonso has received critical acclaim from a wide circle of readers in many lands, especially as her works become available in translation. Currently her stories have been translated into English, Italian, Croatian, and Icelandic, with translations into French on the horizon.

Another global dimension of her work is that it draws attention to Cuba's humanitarian role in sending doctors and others in the medical fields to developing nations where the need is great. The first story in *Desencuentro* describes the author's experience in just such a mission.

A number of reviewers have given *Desencuentro (Disconnect)* a plural title, Desencuentros, perhaps an unconscious way of asserting that interest in the author's work will continue. Critic Llana, for example, states at the end of her review that this third book ensures that readers will want further "encuentros" (connections) with Alonso's fiction. That certainly seems likely since Nancy Alonso has established herself as an important new voice for Cuban women and Cuban literature in the twenty-first century.